Also by Barry Hannah

GERONIMO REX

NIGHTWATCHMEN

AIRSHIPS

RAY

Barry Hannah

RAY

Alfred A. Knopf   New York   1980

THIS IS A BORZOI BOOK
PUBLISHED BY ALFRED A. KNOPF, INC.

A portion of the text originally appeared in the Autumn 1980 number of the *Kenyon Review*.

The author wishes to express his gratitude to the Research Grant Committee of the University of Alabama for financial assistance given in the course of this writing.

Library of Congress Cataloging in Publication Data
Hannah, Barry.
Ray. I. Title.
PZ4.H243Ray [PS3558.A476] 813'.54 80-11195
ISBN 0-394-50972-2

Manufactured in the United States of America
Published November 14, 1980
Second Printing, December 1980

For Gordon, Bill, Elizabeth

RAY

I

RAY is thirty-three and he was born of decent re-
ligious parents, I say.

Ray, I didn't ever think it would get to this. The
woman I love and that I used to meet in the old
condemned theater and we would wander around
looking at the posters and worshiping the past, I
just called her Sister like her parents, the
Hooches, did. Her mother lives in that house with
that man. Her grandmother was a Presbyterian
missionary killed by the gooks.

Ray, you are a doctor and you are in a hospital in Mobile, except now you are a patient but
you're still me. Say what? You say you want to
know who I am?

I have a boat on the water. I have magnificent
children. I have a wife who turns her beauty on
and off like a light switch.

But I can think myself out of this. My mind can do it. It did it before, can do it again, as when I was pilot of the jet when I was taking the obnoxious rich people in their Lear from Montreal to New York to Charlotte to Pensacola to New Orleans to Mexico City to the Yucatán to Tuscaloosa, Alabama, because they had an old friend there.

You can do it, mind and heart. You can give it the throttle and pick up your tail and ease it on. You can do it, Ray.

For instance, look at this male nurse. He weighs three hundred pounds. He's got flab in his eyes, but he used to weigh four hundred. Now he's divorced his second wife and has no remorse and is moving to Key West for a higher-paying job. He has no care for other people because his own elephantine system keeps him employed. You would fire him, Ray. Except you can't fire anyone now.

Nether. That's a good one. Hang on to a word like *nether*.

Her nether hoot. No, I don't, nether. This is the netherlands and it will nether get worse. That is the awfulest netherest laughter.

I just threw up my netherest soul. There's nothing left, nether. My eyes are full of yellow bricks. There are dry tiny horses running in my veins.

That was three weeks ago, Ray. Now I am clean. My head is full of light. I am a practicing doctor again and it is necessary I go over to the Hooches.

My heart, my desire. Sister!

The stacked tires, the station wagon half-captured by kudzu and ivy, the fishing boat on wheels, the tops of an ash and a pine rising from the falling ravine behind the backyard, and in front, the house, a peeling eyesore, the complaint of the neighborhood. The Hooches!

The Hooch children are afraid. The car seems to have plunged up from the ravine. The smaller Hooches are fearful.

The roof of the garage has fallen in and around it clay pots are scattered through the lustrous ragged fronds.

The Hooch family is large and poor.

I have seen the moon make an opaque ghost of the backyard, and I have seen the Hooch animals roam out into it, smelling the life of themselves. They enter the border of visibility and pass through it into the uncanny.

Time and time again it comes back. Where the Hooches buried Oscar in the backyard near the fallen garage. Where the broken flowerpots were pulled away to make a place for Oscar. Where a single white wild blossom occurred under the forever stunted fig tree, making no sense at all, certainly not to dead Oscar.

The others of the street are not of their homes as much as the Hooches. The loud and untidy failures of the Hooches pour from the exits. Their broken car is on the curb in front, pasted over with police citations. Around the base of a ragged bush near the front door is wrapped an old rotten brassiere. In the small front yard parts of toys and soaked food lie. A rope hangs from a second-story window. The drainpipe has been beaten out of place by the children.

The Hooch family has a familiar, I am saying, a certain familiar joyful lust and ignorance. They are mine. They're Ray's.

I say they are mine.

"Hi, Doctor Ray. You got that morphine for me?" says Mr. Hooch.

"Sure."

"I do like that fog."

Mr. Hooch climbs up on his crutch.

"I guess I'm a fairly worthless bastard, aren't I?" he asks.

"You are. You've perfected it," I say.

The old man is tickled.

"Are you horny, Doctor Ray? You want me to call Sister?"

"No, thanks."

"There's nothing to drink. I've drunk everything there is to drink." Mr. Hooch throws out a cough, very nearly pukes. Revives. "Didn't you say you used to be a drunkard, Doctor Ray?"

"I did," I say. "Almost got kicked out of the trade for it."

I can see it makes the old man feel better to

hear it. "Ray," he says. "Ray, boy, that old morphine is sudden, hey? I'm fogging away."

"Your leg already better?"

"Already. Listen to this, Doctor Ray. I know life all round, up and down. I have become my dreams. I have entered the rear of Mother Nature and come out her mouth, and I am the sin that is not ugly."

"That's fine," I say.

"It hurts my leg to talk like that," the old man says.

From the back of the house, looking over the fishing boat and past it to the wide, brittle leaves at the crown of the unhealthy magnolia, there comes Mrs. Hooch with her Pall Malls, a blotched woman in a bravely colored wrap, her legs lean and veiny. She arrives out of breath. She sits in the flaking chair.

"What are you looking at, Doc?" she says.

"Everything in your backyard looks hungry," says I. "There's a bird that looks like he doesn't know what to do."

"It's all we got."

Looking out at the unhappy foliage.

"Ever since I wasn't a virgin no more, things have slid down," she says.

"There must have been love or something," I say.

"Sure, but it was all downward."

I say, "Are you hopeless?"

"Close," she says.

"Well," I say, "I brought another bottle of Valium."

"The preacher was here," she says. "He couldn't do anything. I told him every time you came you left us happier."

"God bless the pharmacy," I say.

Outside, there are two small heads wobbling in the fishing boat. The Hooch twins, the young set. They have older twins too, and three children between these pairs.

"You want to talk today, Doc?" Mrs. Hooch wants to know.

I say, "I get tired of people. All of them driving around in their cars, eating, having to be. All of them insisting on existing."

"But you help people," Mr. Hooch says.

"I'm one of them," I say.

"If you're sad, do you want to see Sister?" Mrs. Hooch says. "I think she's still in bed."

"Maybe I will," I say.

Sister is always in love with somebody, sometimes me. There is a capricious wisdom she has about attaching herself to anybody for very long, although her loyalties are fast. She plays the guitar well and has a nice voice that she keeps to herself. Life has been such for her that she has no attitude at all. She expects no sympathy. Two of her teenage lovers died in an accident at the railroad tracks. That's when I met Sister. I rode down to the tracks, and she was standing there in a long sleeping gown, two weeks after the accident.

"What's wrong, girl?"

"I growed up."

"You want to go home? I'm a doctor. The preacher called me. They're worried about you."

"Ain't nobody should worry. I'll be here."

"I can give you a pill."

But she said to leave her be.

So I drove back to the fancy rich thing of my home in my Corvette. In back of my house is the swamp, where all the creatures are either singing or angry or sexed up. My three well-fed and luxuriously moving furred Persian cats roam around with their big eyes. The back door was open and in front of one of their feed dishes there sits a mother raccoon. She's got two little raccoons with her, who are having a really good time. One of the cats tried for them, but I kicked it back through the kitchen. "Listen," I said, "I am the emperor here. I reign."

Ralph and Robert, my rich brothers, approve. But because of them, I can't even say my name.

But then I had to go back, to see Sister, to see if she's still there at the railroad tracks.

She was. Her gown was wet with tears and she was shivering bad.

"Nothing'll help," she said.

Henceforward we were together.

"Sister, do you have a real name?" I said.

"Sister's enough," said she, "but my real name

is Betty, and my age is eighteen. My grandmother was a Presbyterian missionary, but the Chinese Communists killed her. My pappy's from Mississippi. He ain't worth nothing, but there he is. He never worried about too much and his words is always kind. It was hateful for him to get shot in the kneecap in World War Two. But there he is. I don't want to talk about my momma too much because I don't like her. Her name's Agnes and she acts like that name."

"Well," said I, "I did my part in hurting the gooks back for you, Sister. I flew support missions for B-52 bombers in Vietnam."

"You flew what?"

"An F-4, called the Phantom. It's a jet airplane."

"I've seen them jets pass over me and thought about them," Sister said.

Her figure and face were lively and charming. Her legs were open, dark-skinned, negligent, as in the posture of lust. She had Cajun blood from her mother. Her hair was thick and black, and I suppose her beauty was astounding, even in the dirty gown and her eyes red with nervous grief.

I don't feel that good about women anyway, nor gooks, nor sand-niggers, nor doctors, nor anything human that moves, with its zealous raving habits. Then I met Sister and my trust came back, my body was flooded with hope.

"You hear about Uncle Sweat?" she asked me once while we were making love. "He tried to take off a plane and crashed it into the state pen, Parchman, over in Mississippi. They didn't even have to get a judge or nothing. He was already there."

"Never heard about him."

"Last week Aunt Viola was in a rage about Uncle Tom's carelessness and she dropped a chain saw on her foot."

"Terrible."

The thing I like about Sister is that every hurt she mentions, every hurt she has, she gives it back twice in love. She beats the hell out of my wife, who looks like somebody on television.

My town now is Tuscaloosa. I want you to know about some of the people here. My friend Charlie DeSoto, for example. He and his sweetheart Eileen came in, both of them wanting the drug that would help them stay in love without the grinding nervousness they had, because they *were* in love and they wanted to make it stick. Yet they induced tension in each other. Charlie was going for the booze, Eileen for the Compazines and coffee.

The name DeSoto was important, Charlie thought. He's a manager of the soap factory to the south of town and has made happen important steps toward antipollution of the Black Warrior River, into which his factory used to dump all the chemical wastes it had. It killed fish, and generally screwed up the water vegetation for fifteen miles downriver.

R A Y

One night Charlie was waked up by a noise in his backyard. He caught hold of his hatchet, hoping it was a criminal, for his life had been dull lately. But when he went outdoors in the cold air, DeSoto—who was of course the namesake of Hernando de Soto, the discoverer of the Mississippi River who perished in 1542, probably of greed and arrogance—saw there was no criminal. The man in the backyard was not running. He was crawling, almost wallowing, toiling on the brown rye grass of Charlie's yard. The man lifted his face and said, "Listen, friend, I can't take it anymore."

DeSoto considered that for a while, a whole day, actually. Charlie liked considering things. Best of all, Charlie DeSoto liked considering Mr. Wently. Now this Wently was a man who came by DeSoto's house every morning, *every* morning at exactly 7:45. This Wently was a man somewhere in his seventies, and he was regular. But so was the dog, Albert. Albert belonged to two gentle lesbians, Marjorie and Jane. And the minute Wently showed himself on the block, Albert came out viciously and barked. But the old man was never appalled, for he knew Albert was just a loud coward.

DeSoto wanted to kill Mr. Wently, was the problem. He could murder Mr. Wently for the regularity of his habits. Wently had a three-piece suit and sunglasses and a cane. DeSoto owned no gun, but if he had one, he would have killed Wently first thing.

One day it was a glorious day, and the red and yellow leaves were falling all around the street, since it was fall, the dying beautiful season of the year.

DeSoto was reading about the original de Soto according to Rangel, his diarist on the expedition from Florida.

Sunday. October tenth, the Governor de Soto entered the village of Tuscaloosa, which is called Athlacia, a recent village. And the chief was on a kind of balcony on a mound at one end of the square, his head covered with a kind of coif like the almaizal, so that his headdress was like a Moor's, which gave him an aspect of authority. He also wore a mantle of feathers down to his feet, very imposing. He was as tall as that Tony of the Emperor, our lord's guard. A fine and comely emperor of a man.

Hernando remained seated with him a short time, and after a little he arose and said that they should come to eat, and he took him with him and the Indians came to dance. And they danced very well in the fashion of rustics in Spain. At night Tuscaloosa desired to go, and our Commander de Soto told him that he must sleep there. He slept there notwithstanding his reluctance.

The next day de Soto our Governor asked him for carriers and the rest of them he said he would give at Mobile, the province of one of his principal vassals.

Monday. October eighteen, St. Luke's day, the Governor de Soto came to Mobile, having passed that day by several villages and mountains with two Christians slain by Indians who did not take our passing through their village peaceably. The soldiers stayed behind to forage and scatter themselves, for the region appeared populous. And there came with the Governor only forty horsemen as an advance guard, and after they tarried a little, that the Governor might not show weakness, he entered into the village with the chief, Tuscaloosa, and all his guard went in with him. The Indians danced an *areyto*. While this was going on, some soldiers saw them putting bows and arrows slyly among some palm leaves and other Christians saw that below the cabins were full of people concealed.

The Governor put his helmet on his head. He warned the soldiers. Luis de Moscoso and Baltasar de Gallegos, and Espindola, the captain of the guard, and only seven or eight soldiers were present. Gallegos went for Tuscaloosa, but the chief was hidden in a cabin and Gallegos with his knife slashed off the arm of an attacking Indian. Some got to their horses and killed the savages with lances. I was hit thrice by arrows. Women and even boys of four years fought with the Christians. Twenty-two of us died until the other Christians rescued us with the firearms.

At the last, we had twenty-two dead and their fortification was empty. We had killed four thousand of them.

Many pearls and a great store of corn were found.

Tuscaloosa and all his family were dead. We turned the great tall Indian over. A soldier named

Stellus had fired the buss straight through his chest from five lengths.

Sometimes Charlie DeSoto read that passage to renew himself with his old perhaps ancestor. He got neither any special horror nor delight from it, but it reminded him of the adventurous perversity in himself that he cherished.

Then he thought: What was the *it* that fellow was talking about he said he couldn't take any more of?

This was a friendly city, Tuscaloosa, though there were sirens to be heard most parts of the day and the state asylum across the way was full. On the streets you might see such as this: a small man wearing a football helmet, walking in front of a man in a black suit and white Panama hat, the larger man in black frequently striking the smaller one over the helmet with a broom handle. They were inseparable companions, and the man in black always tipped the clerk five dollars for a Coca-Cola at the Jiffy Mart.

But we were talking about this time in the morning, 7:45. And here comes Mr. Wently by DeSoto's house. This time DeSoto more than ever wanted to slay Mr. Wently. Wasn't there an old bow and arrow in the house somewhere? The hatchet—where was it? Quick!

The dog, Albert, from the lesbians' house attacked. But Wently's routine allowed him nothing but routine, and DeSoto's rage allowed him noth-

ing but passion. It is terribly, excruciatingly diffi-
cult to be at peace, thought DeSoto, when all our
history is war. Look at that whining half-poodle,
half-schnauzer Albert. Half-bred to sit at home,
look elegant, and eat and fart. Half-bred to throw
its vicious teeth into the unknown villain. Wently
is killing everything.

DeSoto called in to the soap factory to say he
was sick, which was true. He was sick with
thought. He lingered awhile, watching a few jog-
gers pass his house—healthy, harmless, in love
with the thought that health promised the whole
thing—bigger breasts, penis, chest. *Endurance.*
That's it. If you can cut through it with peace and
joy. If you can give health to those around you.
But DeSoto didn't feel like it just now.

I want Wently, thought DeSoto. I want to pur-
chase his death.

Maybe there are worse guys than me, he said
to himself. For example, the guy from Minnesota
who hummed all the time. He seemed to be fur-
nishing the score for every puny adventure of his
life. Always the hum, tunes various, dense, thin,
largo, allegro. A trip to the café would take him
through a sonata. There was a tune for feeding
his cat, another for his goldfish, another for wa-
tering the plants in his crummy color-clashing
apartment. He had no radio or phonograph. His
time with women was limited—by them. But on
he hummed incessantly, arrogantly, until somebody broke his mouth at a graveside ceremony

one afternoon. DeSoto played Ping-Pong with him once. The hum was infuriating. They were odd tunes, nothing familiar. This man's game was mediocre, but it must be sung about. Every gesture must be styled by the hum, every blazing inconsequential adjustment had a song. Maybe he had been to too many movies, watched too much television. But the hum incensed Charlie DeSoto even more than Wently incensed him.

He got out his French horn and played a few quick scales, then an inventive cadenza, to impress himself with his culture.

The next morning there was Wently and there went Albert pretending to be at him again. DeSoto was sitting on his front steps reading the paper and Wently passed within three feet of him.

"Hello, damn it," said DeSoto.

The old guy neither replied nor missed a stride. The cane clicked, the shoes, which were rubber-soled, flapped through the leaves on the sidewalk.

DeSoto went to the soap factory, but he was in a state. The workers under him wondered what had happened. He drank on the job, cursed, was loud and impatient, lit and stomped out many cigars. A handsome young man of thirty-four, Charlie was beheld a despot of years. Usually a well-groomed and soft-spoken fellow, today he wore slovenly pants and shouted.

His girlfriend, who was Eileen and was his

secretary, almost called the doctor, who was me. But instead she locked the door to the office and faced Charlie.

"I've got something temporarily that not even love will cure," he said.

The next afternoon he walked around the block to see where Wently lived. He had never known exactly. It was a tall green house with a splendid porch. Wently was rocking in a rocking chair, pushing himself with weak jolts of his cane. He was wearing the three-piece suit. He must have been a man of some means. Big oaks and an enormous magnolia comforted his yard. In a chair next to him rocked a younger man who held his face in his hands, as if in anguish. Wently, decided DeSoto, was also driving this fellow crackers. The two were not speaking. Wently was staring ahead serenely, fascinated only, it seemed, by himself and the system of his rocking—not even by the weather, which was medium blue and fine.

DeSoto observed the grief of the younger man —Wently's grandson? his nephew? Then he walked back home and inquired among the neighbors. It was Wently's grandnephew. DeSoto had been in there right on it.

At 7:40 the next morning DeSoto began his own walk around the block. He was wearing a headdress, cheap, from the K-Mart, and he carried his French horn with him. From thirty feet away, he saw Wently coming toward him on the walk. Should he? Yes. DeSoto played a chain of blats in the high register. Maybe Wently was deaf, but he was not blind.

Anyhow, the old man just passed him.

"Jesus!" cried DeSoto.

A woman professor he knew was just leaving for work in her car, and she saw and heard it all. I'm making a donkey out of myself, thought De-Soto. For the rest of the day he could not eat, and he practiced self-abuse in all possible ways, sort of living in the toilet at the soap factory, moving from stall to stall so as not to invite the looks of the curious and their hellos and how-are-yous.

In the night DeSoto studied gentle thoughts. He attempted to dream of his sweetheart and her delicate parts; of light pleasures he had known, such as reversing the clock an hour when daylight saving time was over; of healthy food; of morning light on the small green ears of corn in his patch last summer. He hummed the placid tune "Home on the Range" several times through. But sleep would not come. He poured himself a tomato juice and took five B-complex vitamin pills, which were supposed to be settlers. But eventually he found himself sitting furious and awake in a chair that faced the window to his backyard.

He was there an hour, through some ten stale Lucky Strikes he had found in a drawer, when he saw the figure slough across the fence in the light of the moon. There was no doubting it was a man, a whole man. DeSoto watched him roll onto the earth and begin squirming on down the lawn. De-Soto was transfixed by the man's progress. When he saw him reach the driveway, DeSoto stood up from his chair. He hurried out before the man could reach the next yard.

"What's with you, fellow?" demanded DeSoto.

The man rolled toward him. DeSoto recognized his body, perhaps his face from their first encounter, the set of hair and forehead from their second. It was old Wently's grandnephew. The neighbors said his name was Ned, a namesake of Wently, who was Edward. Ned was around thirty, but his face was haggard, his eyes heavy with bags and his mustache scraggly and askew, as if false and pasted on at a wrong angle. DeSoto had brought his flashlight.

"I say, what's going on?" he asked again, as Ned Wently blinked his eyes in the light.

"I'm *trespassing,* señor. Better let me have it."

"What's this *señor*?"

"Aren't you Spanish?"

"It's a lie," DeSoto said. "Now answer my question."

"I finally let him have it," the Wently fellow said. "He never knew what hit him. They took away my liquor, my dope and my piano, and they sent me to live with him. I'm interviewing for one dumb job after another. Got one tomorrow at the fucking *soap* factory. That hideous, fucking soap factory that's screwing up the river?"

DeSoto switched off the flashlight.

"Let him have it, did you? Never knew what hit him? Come see me. I'm a foreman at the factory."

The younger Wently did not respond. He crawled off the driveway and through a hole in the fence of the neighbor's yard.

"Why are you *crawling*?" Charlie called after him, to no use at all.

DeSoto was early on the job, at 6:30. He had to open a lot of the doors himself and his only company for a while was the maintenance and sweeping crew. The fumes of the place were violently sweet and sour. He was hungry, horny, happy, and handsome, and he made up a chant to life and himself. I am Charlie, he sang. Hai hai, hai, hai hai, hai!

Charlie DeSoto had had no sleep, but he was elated. He sat behind his aluminum desk, speculating on the gross points of the homicide. *Let him have it* would indicate a gun, or maybe poison. Truly, it could be anything when you put it together with *Never knew what hit him*. Ned would cover it. DeSoto would help him if he had to.

Eileen arrived earlier than usual, and she was all worn out. The old DeSoto car, which she had bought just as a flirting joke to please Charlie—though the orange leather interior was nice—was smoking and stalled at traffic lights. And the driver's door would not open because of some fault in the lock.

She was confounded and thrown into a perilous dither by Charlie's alterations. Moreover, she had cheated on DeSoto the previous night. The man was not nearly as handsome as DeSoto, but his desire for her was constant, soft, a genial tribute to the shrine of her body, and she recalled even the Bible said that was okay. She had allowed the man everything. Now nothing assuaged her guilt. Poor Charlie, poor Charlie, she muttered, sleepless and insane with contrition.

She had to arrive early and make his appearance at the office comfortable. Also she was very erotic, and her satisfaction was not close. She had driven by Charlie's house earlier in the morning. He was not there. The mystery was compelling a storm of expectation. Here was his car in his parking slot at the factory. She hurried in, her body showered but slick again with a new sweat of the day.

She looked pretty and clean by the time the plant air conditioning had cooled her down. DeSoto responded to her chic wool skirt and satin blouse, and, as always, her dark trim ankles and sandals. She was about a quarter Lebanese and it seemed that all the best traits of that race had sprung up in Eileen suddenly.

They were alone in the office.

What happened behind the locked door was

sacred to them both. It was a drunkenness of the bodies. DeSoto was charming and expert at his job, as was Eileen, and DeSoto could bear the fact that, minute after minute, Ned Wently did not appear for an interview with him. DeSoto had looked up a real job for him. It wasn't a make-work job. Ned would have a small, quiet office near the truck docks, a supervisory position. Something higher than he should be hired at, really, but DeSoto would bring in the muscle to make it possible.

As for DeSoto's early morning, it was exalted by the absence of old Mr. Wently on the sidewalk at 7:45. The day was clear and merry without him. DeSoto met the loud bark of Albert with an understanding smile. He also saw the pet monkey come out of Lester's house next door. DeSoto went over and took the morning paper out of its paws, speaking to the monkey, whose name was Amy, in monkey whispers, and taking the nice animal back to his own kitchen, where DeSoto made a huge breakfast. He peeled a banana and opened a can of sardines for Amy, put them on a plate with a napkin nearby.

There was nothing about a death on the block in the newspaper.

Now the office door was locked and DeSoto was near to entering Eileen, with her skirt around her blouse and the tops of her stockings close to her sex. Charlie adored this half-clothed demonstration of lust almost better than anything. There was a call in, however, that a Mr. Ned Wently was waiting outside to see him.

Eileen stood off to the side. She shivered when Wently came in.

He was garbed in a rough tweed suit. His hair and mustache were combed a little, but he still looked disoriented, worse in daylight. The bags under his eyes were dark. His shoulders were wide, but his legs were bowed and thin. The stain of some red sauce was on his neck.

Wently looked at Eileen. His eyes lit up with the normal sex-crazy look of a man. But then he threw his weak gaze at DeSoto, and Eileen left the room.

They sat down, DeSoto and Wently, the desk between them, and were quiet for a spell.

"I've got something for you," said DeSoto at last.

"And I've got something for you," said the younger Wently.

He pulled out a small silverish .22 automatic pistol. DeSoto regarded it. It looked like the foetus of firearms.

"You let him have it with this?"

"I didn't even have to after you scared the fuck out of him with the headdress and that horn. He already had a big cancer and heart disease. You took him to the edge, man. With peace and routine, he would've lived forever. So I never had to fire a shot. Just pointed it seriously."

There was a long silence.

"Then all we needed was the ambulance." Wently's eyes were welling with tears. "Thing is, he loved me. He willed everything to me. I broke his heart when I pulled this thing on him."

Wently began openly weeping.

"But he owed us one, my daddy and me. My daddy was swamped with debt and in precarious health when he was supporting us and my granduncle Edward. Edward didn't always live in that big green house, you know. He's sucked off the family with his goddamn routine and righteousness for years. Until he had his own stack of green and a place. Tell you what, man. These people, these peaceful people leave as many bodies behind as those big war copters in Nam, where I also had to go."

"Then you feel justified?" said DeSoto.

"No!" Wently stared at DeSoto. Then he bent and put his face in his hands, as DeSoto had seen him doing on the porch of the Wently house. "I feel awful guilty. I put him in the ground."

"Come on. Get out of it," DeSoto said.

"*You* get out of it, DeSoto! Have you seen the crap spilling out of those pipes from this puking factory into the river? Where I used to fish when I was a little boy, there ain't nothing but nasty white soap twenty feet down."

"Shoot me in the thigh," DeSoto said. "If you shoot me in the thigh, I'll get you a job," said DeSoto.

"I don't need it. I got his will money."

"Then just shoot me in the thigh. I need some of the pain."

DeSoto put his foot on the desk. Wently shot off one low in his thigh.

Wently went away with a new perspective.

That was all by way of showing you how I come to know Charlie DeSoto and some others. Because I met DeSoto and Eileen in the emergency room. Nowadays, DeSoto fakes a limp, happily. The bullet is in there so deep and harmless and near the bone, cutting for it would be a shame.

Eileen came by to see me by herself later. She was really something to grab, after you got through the usuals. But I liked Charlie and I had rules.

This was all when I was thirty-three and divorced.

11

LAST year I won some awards for my papers at the conventions: "The Nervous Woman and Valium," "Three Seraxes a Day for the Alcoholic," "Satyriasis and Acute Depression." But I quit flying the jets for anybody. Too many pilots around today, especially in the rich class. Some little eleven-year-old will crawl up in the cockpit with you and describe not only the whole panel but continue about your life and your girlfriends, know your astrology sign like the back of his hand, and scold you for lighting up a Kool at the point you'd like to light him up, open his door, and let him deal with the suck at twenty thousand feet.

Ray even teaches a popular night class at the university now. It's open to just about anybody except people I don't like or think I won't. People who work on foreign cars are good. I like botanists and geologists also. These men and women who run from five to twenty miles a day are pretty good sorts. And wrestlers, tennis players. But a category of worst is doctors' children in revolt. Give me an honest nigger any time of day. I'll even read his essays.

I got a little tight and flew right in the sun one afternoon for thirty minutes, and now old Ray has a little eye damage and is very selective about what he reads, which is very little. A man of medicine forgot to wear his sunglasses.

The Hooches are healthier. They've even spruced up their place a bit, but nothing very severe. There's not so much trash around the doors, and their yard looks better, maybe from the fact that their animals have multiplied and the stratum of dung over the grass is near solid. Mr. Hooch has a job and needs very little of the morphine now. I think he's proud of himself as a gimpy tugboat first mate, and he can let his language go wild without worry because everybody else on the boat is bent in the mind too.

"I was saying the other day, Doc, I was telling Poot Laird, 'The large bird flies and roars because it has the span. The small bird creeps and misses because it hasn't.' That's what I told Poot."

"That doesn't sound half-bad," I said. "What was Poot's reaction?"

"Nothing. He can't talk. A cottonmouth bit him in the tongue when he was little. Only expression he's got, is after a big supper and beer, he lifts a leg and——"

"Poots," I guessed.

"But strange, like somebody mumbling."

Mrs. Hooch, Agnes, is happier to see less of Mr. Hooch and have more income. And what she has done with some of it is buy a cassette tape recorder that she uses to record her smaller children, unbeknownst to them, and play it back at supper time to prove to them how much of a dreadful curse they are. She makes them listen to it while they eat. She quit cigarettes, but she's worse than ever. She buys twenty pulp magazines a month and answers all the happiness and sexual quizzes in them. She won a Sony TV by coming in third on a mass-murderer quiz in *Oui* magazine. On the TV she watches Home Box Office movies, which cause her untold anguish for not being slim, twenty-three, in a black dress and pearls, with a submachine gun in her hands, in an old fort on the Mediterranean. She bought clothes and combed her hair so she looks sort of like three decades away from something like that, and I could see Sister's lovely genes in the woman somewhat. In fact, with three ten-milligram Valiums in her, Agnes Hooch is beguiling. Until she opens her mouth, and there are the missing teeth.

I paid for Sister to go to the University of South Alabama in Mobile. She thought she'd like Mobile. But there was no way she could cut college, not even a semester of it. She fell in love with two different boys and they both dropped out too. Now she's a waitress in Atlanta, making a lot on tips and using marijuana by the wagonload. I received a scrawled letter and five one-hundred-dollar bills—her college fee—and a lurid photograph of her in skimpy waitress costume, receiving between her lips the huge member of a fat conventioneer, name badge on his coat, drink in his hand, eyes shut with pleasure and mouth open like a murdered boar. It was made up with the club's name on the bottom. It was clear she was involved in a filthy, lucrative industry. In the letter she wrote:

"Ray, I'm rich, but this ain't me. There's nobody to talk to and I'm turning into hate. Please come and marry me. This ain't me."

I took the next plane out and got a taxi down to the club. I'd always liked Atlanta, and it was grievous to have to despise every building and every bus stop, every mansion and its trees, every club with jazz music and rock and roll pouring out.

But I was Ray, ex–Navy pilot, who used to even have a pistol on me. Old valiant Ray from 1967 to 1969. Gas up, load up, get ready for the worst and give it worser back.

Sister was in Heloise's with two men around her. It wasn't long before she was in the cab with me. The thing was she looked even younger, fresher, long legs in black hose. She cried and we did a lot of kissing. Because of the photograph, I was cooled down toward much gesture of lust for her, though. Besides, I had already met my next wife over in Jackson, Mississippi.

"You ain't going to marry me, are you?" Sister said. "I guess that picture was too much for you," said she.

"Yeah, it went over the line. I can take it in the abstract, but it's not the same photographed. You don't want any marriage thing or you wouldn't have sent it to me."

"You're right, Ray. I just want this."

We hugged in the cab and in the airport and in the plane back to Tuscaloosa.

It was football season and my girlfriend's son was a quarterback for Murrah High in Jackson. Early on, I knew I was in for another marriage, and this one full of love and a slight goddamned bit of wisdom. We went to all the games together

all over the state of Mississippi, and her handsome jock son was the star everywhere. He was a
very cool, light-voiced lad who kept fish, had read
a few books, and took off his cleats when he came
in the condominium on the parquet floors. The
house was gorgeous, snug in shades of blue and
melon, lots of okay furniture around. The ex-
husband was a doctor—Christ!—who was very
busy and very important. Westy, my girl, was
from Iowa, the daughter of a dentist and a corn
farmer who is one hell of a feisty wonderful gen-
tleman. He gets me in a corner and tells these
old-fashioned clean filthy jokes to me. His wife
shrieks and he laughs. He laughs so much he
weeps for sixteen minutes. Westy's brother is an
orthopedic surgeon in Omaha.

There is no escape from doctors. They surround
me as I surround myself.

Westy has an uncommon adventurous warmth
to her, a crazy hope in her blue eyes, and a body
that will keep a lover occupied. I was gone for
her about first sight.

She was forty, had another son off at the University of Wisconsin, and a thirteen-year-old
daughter who received her entire sustenance, by
what I could tell, from her private telephone.
There was also Tina, the live-in maid, an illegal
immigrant from Chihuahua, who cooked Mexican
holistically and, with other Mexican immigrants
in the community, read the Holy Bible every night.
They had converted to Assembly of God and had

nothing for Catholicism and the priests. But the FBI knocked on the door one night when Westy and I were into a little wine and quiet, and the whole flock of Mexicans had to go underground with their Assembly of God friends.

It was a great storm and a great shame. Tina was worth, with her cumin and bay leaf, any ten doctors you can name.

It was a rebirth for old Ray. I hadn't seen high school football since I played it at one hundred and fifteen pounds and one cold night in Crystal Springs, Mississippi, got knocked over a fence and onto a cinder track in the middle of the cheerleaders by some hulking freak who later found his way to the Chicago Bears. That was my last punt return, and I went seriously into Fine Arts after that, where you could play with yourself and get applauded for it. Murrah High was full of blacks now, and you didn't go in the restrooms at the stadiums, where they stayed by the hundreds for the entire game, talked mean, and got themselves numbed out on controlled substances. That is, those who weren't in the band or on the team. The band had an amazing queer black boy named Dean Riverside out in front of them who did more boogie and stretch than the law allowed, the band into "Play That Funky Music, White Boy," and the synchronized Chargettes throwing their legs around the whole affair. They actually made you enamored of the asinine, by God. Such style and earnesty!

One night, when I was in Saigon, a chicken colonel's wife walked past my Yamaha motorbike on the street. My eyes got wide and my heart was molasses. She walked by me, clicking her heels, tanned legs so lean, a fine joyful sense of her sex uplifted at the juncture of her thighs. Her face was serene, her eyes were blue, and she was, as they say, music. I recall the Rolling Stones' "Lady Jane" was pouring from the door of the nearest bar. But she was not mine. I could never have her, and my heart was broken. The image of her kept me pure for years. I resisted the whores in Saigon, mainly out of a horror of VD, and never cheated on my first wife, mainly because there was nothing I ever saw like the chicken colonel's wife again. Until I met Westy.

Westy does not talk much about the act of love. She just does it with all her heart. Her children are beautiful and polite, and she has never threatened suicide, which my first wife was good for at least once a month, maybe thinking her period entitled her to it. We're all God's creatures, but some of us can be especially ugly. I had from this union three beautiful children to present to Westy. She liked them, and the second night we were together, with my two youngest heavenly blessings running around, Westy said, "I want you and all of it."

"Hey, Doc, I hear you're getting married," says Mr. Hooch.

"That's right."

"You look happy and good, Doc. Me and Agnes wanted to invite you to have the wedding right here at the house. We'll clean it up and the preacher will be free."

"Thanks. I got a lot of sentiment for the place, John, but this lady is really fancy and I'm afraid it's going to have to be at the old Episcopal Church."

"Well, could we get invited?"

"You didn't get the engraved invitation yet?"

"I don't know. I don't read much mail."

We went out to a heap of circulars, letters from the police, utility bills, pamphlets from the Cancer Fund, and unread newspapers in the front hall. I picked through it awhile, but I couldn't find the envelope from Westy. Then there was a shriek from the top of the stairs. It was Sister.

"I've got the cocksucking invitation up here!"

Mr. Hooch looked very sad.

"She ain't right, Ray. She sings at night and smokes that marijuana all day and don't eat much. Go see to her, if you would."

Her room was well set up. She had an expensive stereo system with Devon speakers, a microphone stand, a Martin guitar on the bed, which was brass and costly, a thick oyster-shell carpet on the floor, a tape deck, rugged white thick curtains on the window, and the walls were solid acoustic tile as well as the ceiling. It was a studio. It smelled like she'd lit ten joints about eight seconds ago. It had its own refrigerator. The door shut behind me as if in a vacuum unit.

Sister was wearing only panties and a red halter. I'd never seen her look better. Actually, in good light, I'd never seen this much of her.

She had the invitation from Westy in her hand and sat on the bed.

"Ray, you told me once that you needed to make love twice a day or you got very tense and had headaches. But I need it four times a day and I'm getting to be a better singer every day."

I didn't say anything. I was still taking in her and the room.

"There's a man with a glorious voice I sing with named Marcel Smith. We do duets and we are making a lot of money around town and we might get an album contract with some people up at Muscle Shoals."

"That's wonderful," I said.

"Just like your marriage," Sister said.

"I've got this woman. You'd like her," I said.

"I probably would. What do you want to do?"

"Find it and live it," I said.

"Don't you want me too?"

"If it wouldn't be too much trouble," said I.

III

AFTER a Ray kind of honeymoon in Florida, where I composed myself as a father and husband, children from seven to twenty running around my mind and knees, I get a jet, the DC-8, a lovely bird that flies a lot of people, and sit back and dream until La Guardia in New York, queen of the Eastern shore.

At Columbia University there are fifteen doctors, three from the South I know, alcoholics themselves. I read them my paper. I get the applause and the check.

(I have another paper on women, unfinished. Like Freud, I threw up my hands.)

Columbia University got me a companion for dinner at the Russian Tea Room. She was Laurie Chalmers, a Jewess with large bosoms, very visible in a velvet dress. She was a tall, frank girl. After the meal we went back to the room they gave me at the Cornell Club, where Laurie Chalmers disrobed and lay on her back on the bed and described herself as constantly starved—for food and liquor and Southerners. Her family was in Charleston, South Carolina, and she said she missed the South despite her job, that was high-paying. She was an anesthetist.

She was a gorgeous and restless lady, with an amazing amount of beard around her sex. While she talked to me, she chewed a corner of her pillow. Her feet were perfect and unlined and unknobbed in any way. She ate me, just like another delicious thing on her menu. I felt rotten, cool, and unfaithful, yet I came with an enormous lashing of sperm, which made her writhe and lick. Then Laurie Chalmers fell sound asleep.

Ray, listen, I said on the plane back. You don't have the spiritual resources to cheat on your wife. You feel wretched and sinful and hung over, without having had any liquor. Adventures in sex are just not in your person anymore. You know too many people already. Your conscience is banging your head off and you can't even eat your eggs.

So I ordered a double vodka to hose down my conscience.

The idea to keep at it came on, but I beat it back with thoughts of Westy.

Westy fixing up our house in Tuscaloosa.

Westy with her big blue eyes.

But this lousy barnacle of unfaithfulness would not leave my mind. It is enough to be married to a good woman. It is plenty.

Ray, the filthy call of random sex is a killer. It kills all you know of the benevolent order of your new life.

Then the plane is in trouble. The bad things in my head have passed through the air and gone into the engines of the DC-8. Starboard engine is gone, finished, and the plane begins rolling. The stewardess loses everything. Her poise is all gone.

So I go up in the cockpit. One of the pilots has fainted. They're young boys, about twenty-eight.

"Want me to take it?" says I. "There's no big

disaster," I say. "Keep the nose up, asshole. Keep the nose up. Yes. Pull back all the way. What's wrong with him?"

"We've never had any trouble before."

I get the fainted pilot out of his seat, and while the other boy is leveling it, I try to get some action on the bad engine, meanwhile putting in my order for a second double vodka.

We're headed the wrong way, but that's okay. We set it down in Birmingham. Suits me. I didn't have to get another plane to Tuscaloosa. I called Westy and she came over to pick me up.

"Ray, are you all right?" asks she.

I asked her to pull over so I could get out and vomit.

"Darling. Did you drink liquor in New York, darling?" she says.

"Yes. I violated my rules," I say. "Darling, let me have a piece of your Big Red gum."

"I missed you, Ray," she says.

Says I, "I missed you, Westy, in the worst way."

She is such a clean German. The car is clean. I invent cheerfulness from my heart, the biggest engine.

"Ray, there's something else wrong. Not just the liquor," Westy says.

"There's nothing wrong," I say.

"There's something you should tell me. Something's with you. Something's lying heavy on you."

"Basically, Westy, I would like, after we say goodnight to the children, that you sit on my face and let me lick your thing. Like on the honeymoon."

"Oh, boy," she says.

Westy is so happy. Her feet are moving this way and that way over the car pedals.

Sweet God, there is nothing like being married to the right woman.

I V

WE have come up in a meadow, all five hundred horses. We are in the Maryland hills and three hundred yards in front of us are the Federals, about fifty of them in skirmish line. What they can't see are the five Napoleon howitzers behind us.

Jeb Stuart is as weary as the rest of us, but he calls for sabers out. Our uniforms are rotting off us. It's so hot and this gray cloth is so hot. There is a creek behind us. I dismount and we send the orderlies back to the creek. It is delightful to see them bring water back to the horses and me. The water is thunderously refreshing, though you can't drink too much if we have to fight. I would prefer not to fight them, but I can see they've rolled in a cannon and mean business.

Thing is, all the blue boys are going to die. And

we have to do something quickly or they'll tell General McClellan where we are.

Stuart says to me, "Hold two hundred horses with you, Captain. Let us start the cannons and I will go forward."

Then we kissed each other, as men who are about to die.

Our horses covered the howitzers.

They let off theirs. It hits in the trees. These are fresh boys. They don't even really know how to shoot. Yet all of them must die.

I say, "General Stuart, I can kill them all from here. I suggest we don't charge."

He made the order to hold the sabers up.

"What do you mean?"

"Observe us, General."

We had captured an ammunition wagon and it had the twenty-pound shells in it. You could hit a chicken in the middle of the head from this range.

"Do it rapidly, Captain."

I make the order. The cavalry feints to its left. The Federals are confused. Pellham fires the howitzers.

Ooooof Oooof Ooooof Oooooof Ooooooof.

Then again. Five of them are left, and all wounded. One older man is standing up, living but bewildered, with all his friends dead around him.

"Hello, friend," I say.

"Are you Jeb Stuart?"

"No. I am his captain," I say.

"It was too quick for us, Captain," the man says.

Then the banjo player came up and we drank their coffee and ate the steaks on the fires. We threw earth over the dead. Stuart went out in the forest and wept.

Then all of us slept. Too many dead.

Let us hie to Virginia, let us flee.

I fell asleep with the banjo music in my head and I dreamed of two whores sucking me.

V

I LIVE in so many centuries. Everybody is still alive.

V I

WHAT I liked was the tea and bridge club. There were a lot of people around, beautiful young women and handsome men, young and old. It was a large living room in a mansion, and they threw the curtain back after the bridge was over. Husbands and wives were naked in different positions. It was like a dream. A soft-spoken woman asked us to go up on stage and remove our clothes. We were a little bit ashamed. But once Westy and I were into the act of love, we could not help it. There was a woman in real estate. She was wearing a violet gown, high-heeled silver sandals. She had a lecture stick. She did a lot of pointing with it at Westy and me. She said Westy and me were the newest thing.

When I had given my sperm to Westy, the audience stood up and applauded.

Good old Tuscaloosa.

V I I

THERE is Ray's son Barry, a boy with a sweet brain and only fifteen.

There is Ray's sister, Dorothy.

There are Ray's parents, Elizabeth and Bill.

There are his nephews, Ken and Taylor, and his brother-in-law, John, another doctor and a good one.

V I I I

How about we have us a nature walk? The trees, the mountains. Or let us dance at Lee's Tomb, the cavernous saloon near the river and the docking port for trucks.

Sister was there, as were Charlie DeSoto and his girl, Eileen. They are married now. And they look very sad. There is something about marriage that brings on a certain sadness, as if burying the glad part.

Sister is prosperous now that she and Marcel Smith have an album out that is selling big. She has a marvelous suntan and she is wearing jewelry all over her. She looks very self-assured and gives me a self-assured kiss. The Locust Fork Band is playing. That's Asa, Dwight, Bill. God bless you, niggers, for the music.

Besides the small friendly vagina and the blue eyes, Westy has sympathy. We shall be married forever.

Westy, my wife, my darling.

I hate to depend on another human being this much. But nobody is his own boy. Her breasts, her lovely feet, her cheerfulness, her care.

But I still want to fight. I still want to put it to somebody, duke a big guy out. Like the asshole who came in who had shot two of his children and broken the arm of his wife. He was an alcoholic red-neck and had a lot of Beechnut chewing tobacco on him. He really smelled lousy. Before I could ask him anything, he found a razor blade and came at *me,* his doctor! Lucky that Ray still has his quickness. The bastard missed me with the razor, and I kicked him in the gonads.

Certain people are this way. They kill everybody around, for one reason or another. He went to the pen, but I would like to see him tortured in a dungeon to get back the suffering he has caused.

The waving grass of the prairies, the moon settling over Minnesota over the lake. Me and my son Barry are having a good time. It is sunset and there are no loud noises. There are only us, and we've caught some bass and pickerel. My daughter Lee is paddling the canoe for us. Utter fucking peace.

Debbie, psychotherapist, is another person I'd like to see buried. She thinks you get the best out of people when you get them all in a room and ask them humiliating questions. She's about six feet tall and drives her Fiat convertible around town, being queen of the world. She's from Ohio, which is the worst state in the union.

Ohio is silly.

Ken, my nephew, once asked me as we were going to sleep after some snapper fishing in Destin, Florida: "Promise me something, Uncle Ray?"

"What?"

"That when I die I won't be from Ohio."

I X

HERE is something about my class at the university. The pretty faces, the yearning to learn. Deborah, Sammy, Lenora, David, Edward Jurgielewcz, Ondocsin, Triola, Slubowski, Scordino, Edric Kirkman—they are all trying to learn.

The land is full of crashing jets, carbon monoxide, violent wives, and murderous men. There is a great deal of metal and hardness.

The subject of today is breast cancer. Why is there so much of it? Why the mastectomies, why the cancers of the uterus? Why in the hell is there so much cancer today, anyway?

Ray's humble opinion is that it serves us fucking right.

x

OH, help me! I am losing myself in two centuries and two wars.

The SAM missile came up, the heat-seeker. It stood up in front of me like a dick at twenty thousand feet, and the squadron captain told me what the hell was going on. He was a nigger from Louisiana. I think that was the first time a nigger saved my life. Flight Captain Louis Diamond saved my life and I shot the SAM missile out of the air.

Fuck you, heat-seeker! Take some cold steel!

Then when Quisenberry was down on the beach and the gooks were running out to capture my friend from Mississippi, I slowed it down and turned the nose of that Phantom almost perpendicular to the ground. I used the cannons and missiles to clean them away. I saw their heads fly off and their chests.

Tough shit, gooks! You ain't going to get Quisenberry.

He lives now, handsome and a credit to his race, a lawyer in Los Angeles.

RAY

I am very proud of the things I did for my country. I fought for the trees, the women, who, when they quit talking, will let you, etc.

Westy, Westy. It's a miracle.

When we get rid of the carbon monoxide, this will be a hell of a country again. Start with Ohio.

DROP THE BIG ONE ON OHIO.

XI

WHOEVER created Ray gave him a big sex engine. I live near the Black Warrior River and have respect for things.

XII

I'M falling in love with Sister again, who is not my wife. After my breakfast, which I hate to eat but is necessary for the tummy, after the multi-vitamin tab in case I miss something (one of those fuckers might just connect and root me up again), the house is uninteresting and I get out a *Penthouse* magazine. There Sister was, almost exactly. Not her, of course, but right on the button as to looks and smile, nipples, feet. I really find good-looking feet irresistible in a woman. I came near to losing a patient while I was looking at her feet.

She wasn't anything for looks besides her feet. Hubba hubba. I almost fell face-down in her thing while I was doing her appendectomy.

Sister. Listen. I want you. My beloved wife does not seem awfully inspired in the bedroom lately. She's more interested in the house, the yard, wood, and soil.

"I knew you'd be back, Doctor Ray," said Sister.

We were where she sang. The lights on the stage were going full blast. Why the young idiots of today like multiple lights running around and two hundred decibels of guitars and organ, I can't tell. They want to make war out of peacetime. You can't even play Ping-Pong without some young asshole lighting up a pinball machine next to you that sounds like a serious invasion.

Sister quit the set right in the middle and we went to the Hooches and up to her room. She put her feet up for a while and then got naked. Her eyes looked tired a bit. Her toes were chafed by the high sandals she wore. But she was a violent delight. For about an hour we went into the beautiful nowhere together. When she came, she screamed like a man getting stabbed. Lucky that the room was fixed for sound.

"It's not enough," she said after she was relaxed some. "I want it all the way up my ass. Every inch of you, Ray."

She went and got the Vaseline.

None of this should happen, but it does.

"What have we proved?" I ask Sister.

"That it can be done," she said. "I love you, Doctor Ray."

"Sister, I have serious doubts and a filthy conscience."

"Not near filthy enough for me."

There was a knock on the door. Sister began scrambling around for her clothes, as did I. It was Maynard Castro, the preacher. He was a studied man of good will, as far as I knew. There are some good Baptists, and Maynard was one of them. He bade me hello. Then he sat on the bed next to Sister. Maynard had a trimmed beard and gold-framed spectacles.

"I came by to say how much I liked your album. My wife adores it too. We play it constantly. I was going to ask a special favor. You are so admired by the young people in town, I wonder if you'd sing for us at the church during the Youth Impact next month."

Sister lit a cigarette.

"You'd give them peace," said Maynard. "You have given me peace."

"Which song? I thought they were all pretty nervous."

" 'High on the Range.' There is an eerie joy in that tune."

"There ain't any hope in that song. That's about high misery because she's loved too many people. She's about done in, 'cause she spread it too thin."

"I see it as Christlike. It is full of sharing."

"All right, I'll do it."

"I appreciate it, Sister."

When Maynard left, Sister laid out on her back and began weeping.

"I've done it, Ray. I've loved too many people, and now it hurts to love."

Said I, "I've got the same disease, sweetest."

"I need to make love too much."

"Ditto," said I.

"And pretty soon, I want it again."

"There's not much that's truer," I said.

On the way out, I heard Mr. Hooch whistling on the back porch. He must've just come home from work. Agnes was sitting by him in resigned melancholy. Mr. Hooch was swinging his bare feet, sitting on the porch railing, swarthy from his work on the tugboat. Agnes was back on her Pall Malls. I borrowed one from her.

I couldn't tell there was anything wrong with his leg. After the skimpy backyard, you looked into the foliage of the ravine, the car with the wooden Indian at the steering wheel now rotting off the fierce colors of its face. The smaller Hooches, who aren't so small anymore, aren't afraid of that thing anymore either. The grave of Oscar is plentitudinous with heavy white blossoms. It is like a memorial back here, nature doing the main work, going at it in random dereliction with spouts of large beauty here and there.

There has not been time to say that little Con-

stance Hooch had her legs backed over by a school
bus and lost one of them. She is out in the yard
near the ravine, walking peacefully on her artificial leg. She's a ravishing little thing of eleven.
The other twin, Ethel, stays close by, very con-
siderate. They are running down some of the early
lightning bugs with a Mason jar. The older twins
are out front fixing up a broken motorcycle. You
can almost smell the wreck coming on when they
get it going.

Mr. Hooch says, "Guess what I told the foreman stevedore today when we were docking. He's
been long on my list of shits in the world. He's
always nagging about tiny things. He's a big man
with the makeup of a warhorse and the mind of a
shrieking little woman. I told him little certifi-
cates come out his mouth and he ain't got the
wings of a bee."

"That's fine," say I. "That's the way to tell
them," say I.

Some of the white ducks come up in the yard
from the ravine. The twins pick them up and pet
them hard.

This here's the day Dr. Cullen in the History
department has asked me to address the American
Civilization class, because we talked the other
night about Franklin and Jefferson, who were in-
ventors and public helpers, and I have a little
knowledge of them.

So now, class, I say:

"Americans have never been consistent. They represent gentleness and rage together. Franklin was the inventor of the stove, bifocals, and so on. Yet he abused his neglected family. Jefferson, with his great theories, could not actually release the slaves even though he regularly fornicated with one of them. One lesson we as Americans must learn is to get used to the contrarieties in our hearts and learn to live with them." Etc.

I am infected with every disease I ever tried to cure. I am a vicious nightmare of illnesses. God cursed me with a memory that holds everything in my brain. There is no forgetting with me. Every name, every foot, every disease, every piece of jewelry hanging from an ear. Nothing is hazy.

Westy is back. She is developing her entrance into the real-estate profession. She has a dream of being her own person, making her own money. I've never seen her prettier. Yet she's tired. The Westy of the encouraging eyes is tired. At forty-two, she looks as if she's throwing in the towel. Me, I've been visiting Lee's Tomb a lot and taking in too much sound and bourbon. I get up choking. Some mornings I don't even know I get up.

Sabers up! Get your horses in line! They have as many as we do and it will be a stiff one. Hit them, hit them! Give them such a sting as they will never forget. Ready? *Avant!* Avant, avant, avant! Kill them!

Horses gleaming with sweat everywhere, Miniés flying by you in the wind.

Sometimes there is no answer from your wife, even when you're sweet as pie. Sometimes there is no answer from the world. The trees are furry with green, the beach is rolling, the old houses stand straight and thick in the shade of the oaks. And Sister and I are in love.

I read the paper as I was waiting in the emergency room. Sister is dead, and they have Maynard Castro as probable cause. Three times through her precious brain. Maynard just could not take the beauty. Not a sign of sexual molestation. No sign of nothing except an outright shooting in the nightclub where she sings.

He couldn't even wait for her to sing at the Youth Impact.

Lewd stories came out about him, as told by his wife and others. Repressed sexuality that finally pitched him over into total craziness.

Sit on that, Ray. Your left arm is gone.

XIII

THE gulls are coming in to the dock and fighting over the can of sardines I left out for them. I couldn't finish it. I should eat. Sweetest Sister is gone and Westy is gone, and it is hard to swallow a cracker. Out in the gulf you see the edge of your world, many boats, and people falling off, silhouetted by the sun. Arms up, screams, goodbye. The moon is coming in red. Small-craft warnings are out. Over the crumpled horizon the moon seems to roll away the clouds and be a great ruby marble.

Barry and I are here. We aim to catch some fish.

Lee and Barry are also back here in Tuscaloosa with me. Hold old Ray close, everybody, for he is estranged from the clear home that he once knew.

I almost forgot. My dogs are here too. We're all in here now and we are having fun pitching pennies in a minnow bucket. We are about to eat the delicious ribs from Archibald's—happy nigger that smokes them the best—and my daughter Lee and I have had a good time at the university pool. She comes down the slide hollering with glee. She's a water lady of nine years. We go off the diving board together in a backflip. Through the water and swimming forward.

This is me at the trial.

"Doctor, did you ever hear Doctor Castro threaten the woman?"

"No."

"Did you yourself ever have sexual relations with the deceased?"

"No."

"You are under oath."

"The answer is no."

"Semen was found in her vagina."

"Not mine."

"But Doctor Castro has alleged that he saw . . ."

"I'm not on trial here."

Maynard stood up, crying, and confessed. You couldn't understand too much of what he said through the weeping. But there it was. He rushed over to me and hugged me. I came up with a quick stroke from the old Navy practice and sent him sprawling back to his lawyer.

In their secret hearts, such perversities as Maynard know there are things they can never have, things they have wanted with all their hearts. So they kill them. Most preachers are this way. Their messages seem benevolent, but they are more evil than the rest of us walking pavement.

When I fly again, it will be against the preachers.

XIV

AFTER the trial, this man comes up to me. I'm so full of trouble I don't even recognize him. Holy God, it's one of those students I taught in that American Civ class. He wants me to read his poem.

Certain Feelings

I have certain feelings about this room
I have certain feelings about doom
I have certain feelings about trees and gnats
I have certain feelings about this and that

I have certain feelings about firearms
I have certain feelings about the girls and
*   the guests*
I have certain feelings about firearms
I have certain burglar alarms

I have certain strains of Mozart in my soul
Certain helplessness I cannot control
Though I guess when all is said and done
I have certain feelings

They always say Southerners can write. So I slugged this skinny lad. I laid him down the steps. They took this on the local TV, and I watched it with Westy. I was in my white suit and I duked away this harmless poet. He tumbled down a lot of steps and his family is saying they'll sue.

No matter. I'm in Westy again. The thing seemed to have turned her on. Not the violence, but the lonely trouble. Cornelia Wallace called me up about publishing her novel. Fame on the TV got me back to Westy.

She covers me with kisses. Tears running down. Ray heaving, wife receiving. Hear me, poets. I have certain feelings.

R A Y

IN the moon that comes over Dauphin Island, over the bay, we see the gray-blue chariots of the gods move across its face. The wind is running from the south. The night is clear. The blinking lights of the airport tower are throwing out against the color.

The hurricane is over and many people are dissatisfied that it killed no one. Bob the hurricane came in and just sort of raised the water, blew a few phony cupolas off the houses.

Ray meets one of the detestable children of the modern day. I delivered her baby and now she's delivered her modern self onto the world. She was at the 7-Eleven when I was buying crab bait.

"Are you, I'd guess, a Taurus, Doctor Ray?"

"Yes. Nice to see you."

"What are you doing here?"

"Fishing with my father and my son."

"Oh, how macho. Just like a Taurus."

"Yes, isn't it?"

"I'm divorced now."

"Oh."

X V I

WESTY and I are hugging. The thrill goes all around the world. I seem to have made her pregnant. Westy is worried about having a retarded idiot at her age, and we have too many children already. But I want it, moron, imbecile, whatever's in the cards.

Come forth! Take flight! Son or daughter of Ray and Westy!

When the day is done, I have seen ten patients and the sun is setting out over the trees. Westy sits on the bed crying, face in her hands. She doesn't know what to do about the baby. She is scared of it. Another thing to fly and die.

Dr. Ray breaks into tears himself. He washes them away with cold water, but they flood again. The baby in Westy's womb looms up like the huge fetus at the end of *2001*. Our baby, our baby.

Two more days and it turns out she wasn't pregnant, after all. My brain was in squalor and torment. But now it's like another friend I lost in Nam.

"Edward, what you got?"

"I've got something, something on me!"

Then I saw it, the SAM missile go into his exhaust. It was a big white flower spraying in the night. There was Edward, lieutenant commander from St. Paul, Minnesota, a nigger who saved my life twice, falling to pieces. There he goes.

I should have delivered him. I should have been awaker.

Mr. Hooch was at the funeral, of course. Sister was lying all fixed up in the coffin. I couldn't go by to see the body or smell the bank of flowers. Mr. Hooch is a strong man. His wife trembles and smokes. The Hooches have lived in CM (Constant Misery), and now their first claim to fame is dead.

I was shivering. Westy was holding me with her slim arms.

"You really loved her, didn't you?" says Westy.

"Yeah. Westy, I'm sorry, but I did."

"She was lovely. But don't you think I'm lovelier?"

"Yes."

"Is everything just sex and music?"

"No."

"You're awfully down."

"I need more sex and music."

Mr. Hooch shook my hand and said, "We almost had a success with Sister. I told Agnes, 'What the Hooches can't help, they can't help. People born on a bad wind just ride and take it.'"

"That's the thing to tell Agnes."

"We've seen Sister in one way, and now we're seeing her another way. My daughter fell in with the wrong crowd. We all make mistakes. We

didn't know everything about the preacher. He
didn't know everything about himself."

I said, "My God, Mr. Hooch, that's the way to
talk."

He said, "It's my only goddamn talent. When
I quit talking, I'll be as dead as my daughter.
Hold my arm, Doctor Ray. I'm about to fall
down."

We held each other, everything rushing around
us from all corners.

Agnes Hooch has said nothing during the funeral. The heat in the cemetery is a hundred de-
grees and we go out to the hole in our suits and
dresses, hats, sunglasses. The little Hooch twins
have quiet, hallowed looks beyond grief. I see the
maimed one hobbling on her artificial leg with the
hot wind rumpling her dress. She is a vision of
permanent agony. Toward the end of the ceremony Mrs. Hooch raises a dreadful animal wail
of fearful, unknown, soprano lamentation. But
the wooden Indian in the station wagon never
batted an eye.

XVII

LOOK here, you were involved in one murder, says
the voice over the phone, so here's another. I
called you because you've got experience. Maybe
he was a bum, but he was a good bum, and I know
who did it.

I was not involved in any damned murder, I say.

Well, there's a corpse out in Capitol Park, name of Buster Lewis. He's been around a long time. Friendliest, wisest drunk in town. In fact, I'll say it, he was my uncle. I'll meet you there. A teen-ager did it. If you don't come see me, I'm going now to kill the kid with my thirty-eight. Then there'll be two, and I'm on my way to Mexico.

Why me, fellow? There's the police, you know.

Yes, there's the police, but you're cute. Besides, I was a corpsman in the Marines. You get the picture?

Are you a nigger? I say.

Could be, the voice says.

I'll be there, I say.

My Corvette wouldn't start. So I jumped in Westy's Toyota. Edward, Edward, Edward, here I come in this here Jap econo-car! Just hang on.

XVIII

BUT Capitol Park can keep for a while. Let's talk about Judy—Judy and her apartment. She's a lady who ran for mayor on the strength of her large, loving personality. Judy's an honest port. She's not the malicious and bored ground crew. Sometimes there is a true person waiting to talk to you and comfort you, and Judy is it!

I'll tell you, God, you've brought some manure and beauty down on this doctor and aging pilot who saw you face to face over the Sea of China one night, but the blue honest port that he came down to is Judy, who's traveled a bit herself over the herd of crabs in politics. How sweet to be in her place and have her hold your hand.

God makes people like Judy. Poem.

X I X

THERE ain't nobody here and the fog is rolling around. For a moment I'm entering a zone of Edgar Allan Poe privacy. The border of vague in a semi-German or Greek swamp. Rising sins from my past are coming up and haunting my insides, and there's this miserable dew on my buckle loafers. Look here, I'm an important doctor on a mission, I don't have to wait here for creepy phantom business. Then I hear the hiss and the voice.

"Over here, Ray."

"Give me a light."

Out in the park I see Uncle Buster with a bloody face. He's breathing pretty well. But he's in shock. Healthy and large for a wino. I tell the man with the flashlight to raise the feet.

First dawn I have seen in fifteen years, twenty years, twenty-three years. I was a Boy Scout at Camp Kickapoo. I was smoking grapevine in the cabin and Mr. DeLard called me out: "If I ever have to call you out again, Ray, even though you're a Life Scout, I'll have to dismiss you from the troop. You're supposed to be a leader, and here you are smoking."

I have always needed a great exhaust system. DeLard had his Luckies on the top of his knapsack. He was a hairy, frantic man. I went back in the cabin and lit up another piece of grapevine, because I had information. This here was the only time ever I was mean—with *information*. Mr. DeLard ran into the cabin. He had a Scout suit on and was forty.

"Okay. I warned you."

"Leave me alone."

"You're out of the troop."

"No, I'm not! We live next to you, Mr. De-Lard. My dad bought a high-power telescope for my astronomy badge. I turned it around to your bathroom and me and my dad and mother saw you beating your meat!"

Many Scouts in the cabin heard this. It was the first time in my life I'd ever been mean. I was always gentle until people shot at me.

I was a Life Scout, very solid. I knew how to start a fire, eat raw minnows, mold, and worms when it got down to survival. Then I went into Explorer Scouts, which led to flying in the Civil Air Patrol, which led to training on the T-33s in Biloxi, which led to the F-4 Phantom, and I could speak a little French and I was a captain when Edward was gone in the gray-pearl over Hanoi, which is what Tom Wolfe called it, and he was right.

With the Rolling Stones on the tape on my
right side and the whole U.S. hugging my back in
this hot cockpit, I'm throwing off my mask as I
see the MIG-21 come up after the gooks shot my
commander Edward down.

Channel 16. "Daya, menta, menta, casa, casa,
casa, casa, casa!" International jet talk. Telling
the gook pilot to get out of the air or I'll bury
him.

He still rises.

"Vaya casa, vaya casa." Go home or you're
dead, son. I've got everything on me, and this
plane and me will make you burn if you stay up
here twenty more seconds.

But he comes up twirling like a T.

Well, hell. I want him! I turn the Rolling
Stones all the way up, all the states of the U.S.
shine behind me.

He's in the scope. I'm almost upside down and
he's trying to get back home but it's too darned
late.

"You speak English?" I say.

"Uh, yes."

"Are you Catholic?"

"Used to be before Communist."

"I want to know your name and how old before
I kill you."

"Lester Sims, twenty-three, lieutenant, Hanoi
base."

"Lester Sims?"

"Translating. Lu Gut. Trying to fly away."

Then the buttons when he got into the middle of the scope. It's so easy to kill. Saw him make the bright, white flower. It's so fucking hard to live.

Big orange lights in rectangle on my carrier, the *Bonhomme Richard*. Lots of handshakes.

It was the start of what I've got, and no nooky, no poem, no medicine or nothing will make it go away. Jesus, my head!

Six years of medical training at Tulane. They said six to satisfy the med laws. I only had four. But four's all it takes to get the drunk breathing good.

"Shit, he's alive!" I said.

The fellow put down the flashlight.

By God, it was Charlie DeSoto. From the old days of Eileen and Charlie. He had a sad mustache and balding blond hair.

"I knew he was going to make it when I called you," said Charlie. "I've got him and two more uncles in town. This one's a lush and a teenager hit him over the head with a two-by-four. The little punk is over at his grandmother's house and I've got the thirty-eight, like I told you. Eileen has left me, and I really don't care anymore."

I walked over to the house with the light in the parlor. It was four in the morning. I knocked on the door and the grandmother opened it. I asked for the phone. While I was calling for the ambulance, the criminal walked up. He was a big innocent-faced frat boy in an Izod shirt.

"I'll tell you, these scummy winos come out

there and scum up the view of the park. It's more than you can take."

I said, "Bring me the thing you hit him with."

"Sure. Hey. Tomorrow you've got to come up to the Sigma Chi house and have some beers with us. Some of the brothers said you were a keen teacher in Am Civ."

The service answered.

"It's just one of those things," said the student when he got back with the thing.

I bashed the fuck out of his ribs with it and his grandmother screamed.

We put them both in the ambulance.

I healed everybody.

X X

WE wear gray in the big meadow and there are three thousand enemy in blue, much cannon and machinery behind them. The shadow of the valley passes over our eyes, and in the ridge of the mountains we see the white clouds as Christ's open chest. Many of us start weeping and smiling because we will die and we know. Last week we thought we were immortal.

"Shall we charge, my commander, or shall we fall back? We have nothing but our sabers and our pistols, which are cowardly."

"Up!" yells the commander.

You take the saber from your left thigh and

hold it straight above. The pennants go higher. You put the cavalry hat down because the sun is against you. Around you there is nothing because the horses are in perfect line. The sun is coming over the raised sabers.

"Commander, we could fall back. Our horses can run away from this."

There is no turning back. Hold sabers. We will walk to them until they shoot and then we will charge.

Everybody was killed. One Union private lived to tell the story.

If warriors had known this story, we would have taken the war to the gooks with more dignity.

X X I

ME and the machines saved Uncle Buster. He woke up wanting some wine. All ready to be a bum again. Go out there in the park, safe from vigilant idiots who get their haircuts at fifteen dollars.

X X I I

"EILEEN left you?" I hadn't been listening too good.

"For a month now. She didn't like my friends.

She used to be nothing but love. Now she's just complaint and fury. What happens to women, Ray?"

My clinic is on a small offstreet. Through the window I can see the trees waving back and forth as the thunderstorm comes on. Linda Ronstadt is on my tape deck. I turn her down. I was listening more to "Blue Bayou" than to Charlie DeSoto, honestly. One afternoon I saw a gorgeous stag raise his head out of the hedge of yellow flowers. Right here in the middle of the city. There is a creek that runs down to the Black Warrior River and there is a thick swamp as it meets another creek, where there are deer and immense snapping turtles. It's a haunted place, full of tales. Sister may be there now.

"What?" I light up a Vantage.

"I don't understand what happened to her after we got married."

Charlie had acute gastritis over a peptic ulcer. Lots of buttermilk, if you can stand it.

"Look, Charlie. I'm going to stick you with some morphine and I'll drive you home. Drink the buttermilk and sleep as long as you can. But this is the only time. Morphine is dangerous."

"Don't tell me. They used it in Nam."

"Okay. Let us not use the Demerol or any of the other shit after this. We're just going to have to wait and see if your belly comes back for you. It should. A belly does."

"I got a raise. I'm the plant manager now.

There's a girl at the office who's twice as good-looking as Eileen. She wants to lick my dick. I don't know what to do. I'm sick."

"Your blood pressure is up. Knock off the salt. Buy yourself some garlic pills."

"Garlic?"

"Trust me. We'll get them at the drug on the way home. You're the last patient today and I want out of this office. Catch 'M*A*S*H' and make love."

"Why do women change after you marry them? She hates all my friends and is always tired when I try to get it on."

"You want to go fishing soon? My son and I have been catching some nice bass."

"You haven't told me a damned thing about women."

"I tried to write a paper on the subject once. Pick up a *Cosmopolitan* magazine at the drug. Women read it to find out who they ought to be and then that's who they are. A guy whips his pudding when he sees the new look in bathing suits. If Jackie Kennedy sucked you off, your ulcer would go away."

"Can you get her to do it?"

"No," I say. "For doctors, they have Claire Bloom and Lee Remick, but simple street shits like you just have to buy *Penthouse*."

Charlie smiled.

It is always a sign of health when the smile can

rise. His eyes are brighter. This handsome bastard will outlive me, and I resent it.

The nurse comes in with the needle. She's trained in the great med center at Birmingham and she is a knockout. Her hair is blond and curled. She's about five-nine, a tall girl, twenty-six, and her legs are an amazing long event. Beyond that, she's just a straight honest slut. I never had her. It is a perversity, but I hired her just to tempt myself and resist, as a man who's quit smoking keeps a pack of Luckies on his desk just to see what he won't do anymore.

Rebecca puts the needle in him. When Charlie phases out, he lifts his hands in prayer. She looks at me quickly. She takes down the top of her uniform. The large dark-nippled breasts are there. Charlie is lying in the leather chair and she lowers herself to him.

Certain things are private and it is tacky to witness them.

In three weeks his ulcer was cured. He came by the office to tell me how delightful it was to be healthy. He told me he paid Rebecca for a week, but all the rest was free. Eileen was still in Georgia, waiting it out, knowing she was hurting Charlie. Women enjoy revenge more than the worst Apache.

Then sabers up and we knock the fuck out of everybody. With the cherished dream of Christ in our hearts. Basically, the message is: Leave me the hell alone or give me a beer.

Yes, I have seen the rain coming down on a sunny day. I have seen the moon hot and the sun cold. I have seen almost everything dependable go against its nature. I have seen needless death and I have seen needless life. One old mule of eighty came into the emergency room who had abused three wives, beaten his youngest son, twelve, with a tire tool, and had borrowed from everybody in Gordo. He had a heart attack and he was in intensive care, all hooked up to the machines and the monitors. He wanted to talk to me.

"When I get out of here, I'm going to kill all those sons of bitches, Doctor."

I'd brought Rebecca with me. She can bring a man back. She can bring a woman back. A lesbian on Methadone came in wanting to die one afternoon. Rebecca put the bottle up and I straddled her, looked down her throat, opened it, and eventually got a pint of buttermilk down her. Then she was fighting and weird and we had to get the heavy stuff in her. After she was calm, Rebecca took her skirt off and sat on her face and the girl licked her wide hairy organ. I watched this one because I thought the girl might die.

But Ray confesses he deliberately lost the bastard who was eighty. I told everybody to get out of the room and I bent down my face and looked him straight in the eye.

"What are you going to do when I get you on your feet again?"

"Kill the sons of bitches!"

I yanked out the connections and shut down the monitors and let him pass over the light into hell. By the time the crew came in, I had all the stuff going again.

"I lost him!" I screamed.

Rebecca saw me in the hall. We lit cigarettes.

"You killed him," she said.

"Well, hell," I said.

"You want to get it on, Doctor Ray?"

"I can't. I have a wife. Westy."

She said, "I want you to screw me, darling."

"Yeah. But I killed the old guy. Never did that before."

"He deserved it. Let's go dance and fuck."

"I forgot how to dance about twelve years ago."

"Yeah. But we could just go to my place, and fuck. You ever hear Jimi Hendrix? You and I could've saved him, poor old genius nigger."

XXIII

"RAY?"

"Yeah?"

"They got me."

"Contact, Ed. I'm hearing you."

"Put your spirit with mine now, old lieutenant. I'm ashes."

Then he was.

The last time Sister came to me at the clinic, I wrote this record and this prescription.

—Female, 23. She has made one album and her next one is in process.

—Her mother, almost nonexistent.

—Her father, a philosopher.

—Her family. Two sets of twins, one of them recently backed over by a bus, plus two others.

—Her situation. Singer. Uses marijuana heavily. High blood pressure. 150/90. X-ray shows dark spot in the upper left lung.

Prescription:

—Valium, 25 mg. Every four hours until appetite returns. Prednisone, 200 mg. One every other day for two weeks. Then a half-pill every other day. 60 days. No refill.

X X I V

PAT and I go out in my little MG. I don't have the Corvette anymore because of the gas. But I like my little 73 Midget and the sky. You get this low and you get to look at the sky.

So me and Pat go out to the airport to look at the new two-million-dollar Learjet, and we get in the cockpit, and I show Pat the controls.

Pat is a wonderful guitarist from Chicago, as well as a medieval scholar and poet. Nobody's killed him yet.

X X V

EVERYBODY I love is in the jet. We try New York, but it's no good. I've got the .32 machine pistol that I killed a gook in the head with. He was dead and he had a hand grenade in his hand. But he threw a knife into the neck of Larry. We were all fueling at Ton Sa Nut. Fifteen F-4s all in line. You couldn't ever kill enough of them. Vietnam was like fleas.

Never had a whore in Saigon. Never gambled my money. Quisenberry and I mainly just talked ourselves to sleep, then dropped Dexedrine when the horn sounded.

Harry King was flight control one night at the Tuscaloosa airport and brought Don in on auto-pilot from Chicago after he'd turned the plane in a storm and fainted.

Ray is out here with his beeper on his leg, just watching the planes come in over the blue lights, for no reason except to find my meditation again. Somehow the AM waves are getting into my beeper and I hear "Eleanor Rigby" from the Beatles. Where *do* all the lonely people come from? Ray is starting to sound like a man who

was once a disk jockey. Because he's run-down.
I'm full of dopey tears and just as groping and
lousy as the next citizen.

So I just wander into flight control. Harry's
very lonely with all the Teletypes. What in the
hell comes in but an F-4 from the National Guard
in Birmingham. He touches down, then off, wheels
it out, gone at five hundred miles per hour. Beautiful Phantom.

"How you been, Harry?"

"Ray! Goddamn, you're here!"

Here looking at the flat charts of the flight
territory all over the world and Harry, still wearing his tie from WW II. He's driving his crummy
Toyota since the gas crunch and we talk about
that. We share one of those huge TV dinners
made for two. Not much to do here now.

The beeper sounds and it's Rebecca.

"What?"

"Nothing, really," she says. "I handled it. I'd
just sort of like you to run back here and
dick me."

"I don't have it in me," I say.

"Okay. There's another message, from
Westy."

"Put her on," I say.

"I just cured three creeps with a light assist
from your buddy, Doctor Litchens. You can't im-
agine the swine I'm going to have to do a number
with tonight."

"Put Westy on."

It was fifteen minutes. Harry and I were finishing up the chicken on the plate when she called. I hadn't heard a straight and clear message from her in three months.

"Ray? Raymond Forrest?" My first two names.

"I hear you, darling."

"Ray. We can make lovesies again."

"Holy Christ!"

"Yes," she said. "I want to be lovely all over you again."

I was so entranced I forgot Harry King was right there beside me. You never get a whole conversation over the beeper like this unless you got somebody relaying it. Rebecca did it and was listening in.

XXVI

I NEVER woke up feeling better. Made coffee, eggs, bacon for all my six children.

No complaints.

XXVII

THE beeper goes off when Westy and I are doing something. We have our tongues so deep into each other's and I am sucking her beautiful feet. It's Rebecca.

"Mr. Hooch and Agnes bought a propane lantern and it exploded. He's almost dead from burns, Doctor. She has second-degrees."

Hooch was burned to a crisp and he weighed about a hundred pounds. His system was so exasperated, it was a total moan. The protein and the platelets and the nerves were wrecked and closing. His kidneys were going out. His liver count was as high as a man's who hadn't eaten in three months. The calcium was not protecting his lungs. Yet on fruit juice and plasma, his mind stayed. Even brighter. What an organ. You got a third of it left and you can still be a genius. For a while we couldn't even get creamed field peas down him. He was burned down to the condition of the inside of a steak as Texans like them.

"You tried to kill yourself, didn't you?"

"No."

"Yes, you did. You know better than to light up a leaking propane tube."

"I get tired of my wife and me. There ain't much going on since Sister except my mouth."

"Gimme a poem, Mr. Hooch. Let's hear the best."

One of the humiliations of my life was that my own secret poems never touched the poems of this old fart. All his genes must have run a pretty direct route into Sister.

Fire at Night

by J. HOOCH

*Fire at night and it's me. I've been born with
    pain*
So this is sort of the same.
Agnes talks about forty years ago.
*Her love is around, but I never got her mind's
    number.*
Love is above and behind you,
But someday, honey, I've got to find you.
*We bad luck together and it ain't ever going
    to get better.*
We worse when we try to get better.
We got the jinx and the voodoo visited upon us.
But it's New Year, so I'll light myself up
With a cup of gas.
It'll be a hell of a feeling,
And this one will really, really be the last.

"Not bad," I say.

I go back to the dinette and sit with Rebecca.
I smoked about four Luckies in a row and looked
into her face without saying anything for a while.
Rebecca's face is a charm. She goes heavy on the
blue eye makeup. Her neck is a longish classic
from the old paintings of what's-his-name. Her
nose is forward and long. She lights a Lucky and
the exhaust is gray through the large sensitive
nostrils. She's half-Jew, the rest Greek. Okay,

now I've come back from the humiliation of never thinking a better poem than Mr. Hooch. Then we go through two cups of coffee apiece. Modigliani.

"No, he's not, goddamn it."

"There's not much here at the hospital."

"There's the Freon tube."

"They won't let us use it yet."

"I have a key that's copper-colored in the far right on the front desk of the office. There is a forty-five pistol right next to it. Put it, the key, in that little safe. If you can't open it, get a pillow from one of the chairs, push it over the muzzle of the gun, and shoot out the lock. I'll meet you at the hospital."

"The FDA won't . . ."

"Do it, bitch. Move it quick."

It worked. Then I sent him over to plastic surgery.

XXVIII

I BROUGHT a new Goliath harmonica made by Hohner into J. Hooch's room. By then he weighed a hundred and thirty and was looking fairly decent.

"Gimme that son of a bitch. Whose is that?"

"Yours."

A month later he was back at the Hooch house. I would put the MG on neutral to hear the strains coming from Sister's studio. His bed was there. He's moved to it, all the guitars, the stereo around him. The old boy was playing the hell out of the harmonica. He was at a hundred and fifty and going normal.

"I'll be what my daughter was trying to be!"

"What?"

"Already got myself recorded. All I need is a drum. I read Sister's diary! Goddamn it, I'm a great old son of a bitch!"

The dirty dog was playing the harmonica every time I came by the house. I'd just shut the car down and listen to the tender sorrow coming through the forty-eight reeds.

Then with duty on my mind, I go by the emergency room. Nothing. The usual hurt niggers, but all's in control.

I am late coming home and Westy is pissed off. Yes, I had some bourbons, and I guess I just sort of threw her nightgown up and tried to.

Women enjoy conversation.

Lube does not come in before talk.

I got up to brush my teeth and prove I'm not drunk.

All right.

Afterward, I ate her slowly. I hadn't eaten much all day.

RAY

ERD. #92. #Doe4. Utap. At 40–50. Range. In Clear. Solid. Ventro.

X X X

THE other night one of the deranged creeps got out of his car at the emergency room, swinging a Magnum in his hand. He had already swatted his granddaughter in the head with it, plus shot his regular daughter in the tit.

I had been shooting the .30/30 with my boy Barry that day.

I asked him to ride into the back lot with me, because I was a doctor who understood him. Something about my stern eyes that calms even wild men down. He gave me the gun. We got way out there where nobody could hear. I played some country music for him while I pulled a towel over the barrel of the .30/30 and rested it into his ribs.

"What was you going to say?"

"Light up a cigarette for me," I said.

While he did, I let one go through him.

"What'd you do?"

"Let out some of your spleen and piss," I said.

He fainted, of course.

I took him back to the main entrance and kicked him out.

Now he'll live but be warned. I've still got his Magnum.

X X X I

Now I guess I should give you swaying trees and the rare geometry of cows in the meadow or the like—to break it up. But, sorry, me and this one are over.

X X X I I

I GOT audited by the IRS because I hadn't filed in four years.

So I went up there to the Federal house. They had called me over the phone and finally got rude. I tend to procrastinate on business like this because I feel I don't owe anything and already fought for the country. I'm for the straight ten percent. I'd file before anybody then.

She was not so stern when she met me. I had all my forms. She went off in the room and talked to her boyfriend for thirty minutes. I went down to the first floor and got some coffee. Saw a nigger in a Federal suit and asked him if I could try out his gun. There was nothing else to do. Then I got some Nabs. Those are fun. I ate two and spat out the third. Welfare niggers who don't work for a living are all over the place.

Finally she got back to the desk. She had to make another call or receive one.

This was enough. I went back in the other room, raised up her skirt, and stuck the meat in her. She was talking to her boyfriend and moaning.

Now I am clean with the IRS.

XXXIII

ELEMENTS of protein float in. B-12 for sanity, vegetables, and Oscar, the mysterious warrior that sails in the bloodstream. Can be cancer or the warrior *against* cancer. I'm dreaming of this. I'm dreaming of the day when the Big C will be blown away. I'm dreaming of a world where men and women have stopped the war and where we will stroll as naked excellent couples under the eye of the sweet Lord again. I'm dreaming of the children whom I have hurt from being hurt and the hurt they learn, the cynicism, the precocious wit, the poo-poo, the slanted mouth, the supercilious eyebrow.

Then I wake up and I'm smiling. Westy asks me what's wrong.

"Christ, darling, I just had a good dream, is all."

"I'll bet it was some patient you screwed. You rotten bastard."

She hits me over the head with a pillow.

Violence.

Some days even a cup of coffee is violence.

When I can find my peace, I take a ladder to the hot attic and get out the whole plays of Shakespeare.

Okay, old boy. Let's hear it again. Sweat's popping out of my eyes, forehead.

Let's hear it again. Between the lines I'm looking for the cure for cancer.

XXXIV

LET'S get hot and cold, because, darling new thing, we're going through the weeds and the woods and just the sliver of the moon comes in through the dead branches, and the running rabbits and squirrels are underneath and above. Henry David Thoreau is out there thinking, loping around. Louis Pasteur is out there racing with the bacteria.

We went to the planetarium in Jackson, Mississippi, my hometown. Elizabeth, Ray, Lee, and Teddy. Elizabeth is on the couch with her crocheting. Lee is reading her new bible, Proverbs. It's raining out. We've cut the yard in the front, and the train whistle is hooting.

"A gentle answer quiets anger, but a harsh one stirs it up."

"It is foolish to ignore what your father taught you. It is wise to accept correction."

They say, "Dad, take it easy. Quit going so fast."

My daughter has a secret friend named Fred, and my son Teddy has a secret friend named Jim.

We all sleep together in the big wooden four-poster where I grew up, tiny innocent arms and legs and imaginary friends on top.

Ike, Ken, Carol, and Ginger are at my ex-brother-in-law's place, and I join them to fish at the wide kidney-shaped lake at the bottom of their rolling lawn. Dr. John and Dr. Ray trade a few compliments. John would give you the shirt off his back. It's a shame my sister, Dot, isn't with him anymore. There were differences. His wife, Mindy, is sweet and has Buffy and Moffit. I forgot to mention my beautiful nieces, Hannah Lynn and Maribeth. Everybody's around and we are flying kites over the tall oaks, the Black Angus cattle are roaming comfortably in the taller weeds, and the geese control their placid squadrons.

Ike is a playwright and Ginger has just come back from Europe with her Gitanes, one of the essential deeds of young females. Looking back at the house, it's a low wooden castle.

X X X V

THEY asked me where I wanted to go to graduate school and I said Tulane, for medicine. Finished in three years. Or maybe it was four.

X X X V I

ONE of the great bad strokes I did was marry the prettiest girl on campus. I was so horny and everything else was pretty nothing except red bricks and Baptists, a few queers in the drama and English departments. I got thrown out of my room by a senior who thought he could box. I knew nothing about boxing. This was supposed to be my roommate. He was a blond, acned guy, and he was punching me. So I said, "Stop."

He quit, though he was still shifting, bouncing.

"My name's Wild Man Thomas," he said.

X X X V I I

IT's quiet, utterly quiet, except for the air conditioner going in my room. The companionship is with the air alone. I am asking forgiveness for all my sins, on my knees. I got to get my mind in a higher sphere.

RAY

I WAS treating a large old woman who spat in my face. I fell backward into the heater, face-forward. This is to prove that I'm not always the hero.

NURSES have saved me. I wander through the day like a horde often. I can't hit the directional signal on my car. I trip over my unredeemable cockiness. I drop a can of 7-Up in the hall and fall down in front of Dr. Everything, the world surgeon I always wanted to meet and impress.

One evening, late, I was watching a nigger up in a tree picking his nose. The nigger worked for the electric company and was apparently new. He'd climbed up the tree next to the light pole.

"What you laughing at?" said another big nigger behind me, wearing a helmet.

XL

FOR no clear reason Ray will have it out with the plants in his place. His anger comes up when he looks around at the expensive greenery and all the deathly care people give to plants when, if let alone, all plants are fine. Plants can talk, he's heard: "Eat me. Eat me." That's all Ray's ever heard. Anybody besides Ray see *Little Shop of Horrors*? A great plant in some creepy Jew's flower shop starts calling out, "Feed me, feed me!" He eats people. So the Jew goes and accidentally kills a number of people and their faces appear in the blossoms of the plant.

Ray has lost it. He kicks over the plants and yells abuses. Mainly, it's because his poems are not going well and he still can't come anywhere close to old J. Hooch.

Westy comes in. She's disturbed.

"Are you drinking, Ray?"

"No. Get me a drink."

She's wearing beige sandals and her toenails are maroon. She has a glass of milk with her, reaches back with it, pours it over the crease of her buttocks and fetches my tongue in.

I'm as earnest as an evangelist when I mount her.

X L I

BILL, my dad, came over to check on me again. He's been everywhere, from hard-crushing Depressionville to Russia. Got him the new Mercury

that gets twenty-seven miles per gallon on un-
leaded, high visibility. He still looks handsome.
Still the man who gave me life. Seventy-five years
old. Afflicted only by deafness and arthritic feet.
Always got money, maybe pull out a thousand of
the five hundred of them he's worth now.

Bill roomed with Senator Eastland at Ole Miss.
He and the great senator were going to be law
partners. But Bill had to go back to Homewood,
in Jefferson County, to support his family. Bill is
a naturalist and is determined not to let Ray not
listen to his advice now because he never had any
advice for Ray when he was young.

Bill looks good.

He has the open, eager eyes of a man who has
confessed and tried to put it back right. He always gave me the advantages.

XLII

COMING back from the convention in Omaha, I
was thinking about my first wife. Because you
have to be honest. You are packed with your past
and there is no future.

We got married stupid and frantic, Millicent
and me. Things at one point were lovely. The children were lovely, and waiting for them was a
miracle like the rainbow. And although you try
to get shut of those gorgeous moments when we

had nothing but good neighbors, the pines, and the sky to look at, it's true, we had a sublimity. Our children are ready for the world, and they are handsome enough and know enough science.

I have seen so many people not worth saving, not worth putting the tubes into.

God jokes with his best ones.

What release, to look into the past the way I just tried. A petrified log just rolled off my heart.

XLIII

CHARLIE DESOTO is in the office.

"Ray, I've discovered that my wife is a lesbian, or at least so far divorced from usual commerce between us that love words do no good. Lovemaking hurts. It seems to be an inconvenience. It's smelly, messy. She makes me feel like a raper. I can never satisfy her. This baffles this poor fool who married her and had so many, I can't tell you, uh, loves with her. She prefers to sleep with her old coloring books. Nothing sensual I can say to her touches her. I've been drinking too much. I've used cocaine, LSD, listened for the phone, waited for her letters, since we've been apart. What do I do?"

"Split. Get out of this CM."

"But I still have wonderful love dreams of her."

"You can have dreams of somebody else."

"I envy you and Westy. You sit there very smug."

"Get off of it. Westy's a hell of a woman, but I've had three months with no nooky. People are like weather where she grew up. I'm terribly sorry your wife's queer."

I went by Hooch's house. The yard is cleaned up. The backyard is raked and the grass is growing around it like a billiard table. They are clean and neat now that Sister is dead. He's working on the tugboat and looks two decades from his real age. He and Agnes don't sleep in the same room anymore. He lives in Sister's acoustic-tile room, and he plays those records and he writes his poems that beat the hell out of mine.

And the old man is sixty-seven. He's got himself an Olivetti automatic typewriter and plays Sister's album over and over.

He picks up her brassieres and her pictures and her underwear.

He handed me one:

Grief is
Looking at the wooden Indian where your
  little ones should be.
I bought a new color teevee.
All the people you should be are on the screen.
Everybody is pretty.

XLIV

THERE will never be, stepson, another person that
I have respected and loved as much as you.

Your stepfather will not fall down. Your step-
dad Ray has created abuse and horrors in the
house because of him and drink. I wasn't born
straight. God gave me a hundred-and-fifty IQ and
perfect pitch on instruments. Sometimes I don't
hear. I am having a constant burn-out on communi-
cations. Nobody means any harm. Everybody is
swell. Just can't get through to anybody.

You, boy, will travel with beauty. Not just
righteousness, which is easy, but beauty too. I
saw you at Murrah move like a genius. You are a
chieftain. You threw the ball, you scrambled, and
the niggers dropped it.

Never be cruel, weird, or abusive.

I promise not to take a jet anymore.

I love your mother.

Amy, Bobby, too.

This boy is so full of loves the juice comes out
his eyes.

Alt. 2000, 1000, 500, 120, flaps down, lights
on? Yes. Port. Pork and beans.

Pick the football up, travel rearward on your
legs, the way is clear, there is your receiver, arms
up in the lights on the green field. The football

leaves your arm like a quail. He's got it. Runs into the last green zone.

X L V

ARE we here? Is everybody here? I have scored six points, the lights are up, but the stadium is empty. Want to do it again, Westy? Want to get married again? Want to be in the day instead of just walking through it and paying the bills? The deck has gone out from under my legs and we're on the rocks and we're on fire. Handsome craft, pure white, with sails up and now it's not going anymore. She was blue-eyed, white. But now it's raining fire. Everywhere you lift your eyes, a rain of cinders.

You get to the end, and you're still swimming.

The people sing. My heart is all over my front yard. I am still reading Bill Shakespeare.

Bob Moony's here. Mr. Hooch is here. There's no other reason to be in Tuscaloosa.

Mike White is here. For God's sake, where else *is* there? That's why a lot of people are here.

All we have is together.

And sometimes I cure others.

Christ be with my friend Phil Beidler. He has a polyp on his vocal cords. I thought he might have C. Called Ned Graves in Jackson, Mississippi. Best one in the world with the knife on the throat. Phil was knocking down two packs of Marlboros a day. Like me, he loves his ciggies. Called Ned up. He was drunk, but wanted to fly over and get the C out of Phil. But good old Phil didn't have it. Ned's only twenty-eight, works in clear weather. No damned war memories. He just walks in with five knives, and can see cancer with his own eyes. Knifes them off. Only lost two patients in all his time. A nurse was the cause once. She overanesthetized the little boy. Ned went out in the parking lot, put the nurse in the front seat of his Mustang convertible, sat there saying nothing for fifteen minutes. She didn't have a driver's license and she was night-blind—big, thick glasses.

"You killed him," said Ned.

"I wish you weren't so emotional."

"You killed the boy." Ned drew on his cigarette. "Walk home."

"I live in Pelahatchie. That's twenty miles."

"Walk home."

So Ned is there, and I think of Ned. Sometimes it is better to think of your friends.

X L V I

In desperation, I got a little dog named Elizabeth, spotted, three-quarters bird dog, abandoned by some person and running around the parking lot of the apartment where my stepson Tommy lives. You know how dogs are faithful. But she chewed everything. She chewed the shoes, the Oriental rugs, and the windowsills, plus leaving diarrhea all over the house. But her eyes were deep, hopeful, and oozy with affection. Thing is, her existence broke up Westy and me almost. Elizabeth ate a couple of pairs of Westy's sexiest sandals.

Born to chew, apparently.

The feet of Westy are so beautiful.

I finally wanted to get rid of the dog.

The bare feet and the toes in the golden high heels will bring a man on when he's entering his lady. You look at those and hear your woman moaning with pleasure and there's something so deeply elegant to the erotic that you've got to look into *Penthouse* after you've finished making love to be sure it really happened.

So I took the little dog out and kissed her good-bye.

X L V I I

I HAVE talked of pornography and medicine and love of art—which is Mr. Hooch's poems.

Many friends around.

And I work here and crank up the bodies that are slow.

Westy has gotten so absorbed by inflation and

her stepchildren that she does not raise her happy irises to me anymore. She cleans the clothes and makes suppers and if she is not a lesbian, then what is she?

I am drinking five bottles of wine a day just to stay cool. Looking forward to the football at Alabama. I'm not going crazy and am not violent. I could play better tennis if my habit on nicotine would give up. I roam in the past for my best mind.

XLVIII

I HAD a little hashish and some Jack Daniel's, so I went out to Tuscaloosa airport, broke in the hangar, and took up the Pfeiffer Wire Learjet. Wanted to go everywhere. Refueled in Atlanta. Then I was all out of chemicals and had to do it on guts to get near Toronto, over the border. No chance. I was out of fuel, lights were off. So I crashed it in a small lake by the woods. First time Ray ever had a crash. Had his son's new guitar so as to strum along and almost burned it up too.

I walked away from there and the Lear blew up and took away about an acre of pines. I could not believe I lost that much good equipment. But wait a minute. The explosion lifted my son's guitar out of the cockpit, and I saw the bright strings loft over the pines and I ran and caught it.

So I hitchhiked back to New York, where I had a friend. I got a sailboat to outside of Philly. Then I rode a train back to here.

I was black as an Indian when I arrived at the door of my tranquil house. I'd lost weight. I was back to a hundred and forty, as in high school. My lovely, caring brother Robert was in the house, They all had huge eyes, worrying if I was dead.

"Who are you?"

"Your relative," I said.

XLIX

WESTY gave me a roll yesterday. A good one. Toes and all.

Also the phone came in from Mr. Hooch. He's beating the shit out of Shakespeare with his new ones.

L

YOUR hat's rotting off. It's hot. You're not sure about your horse. Or the cause. All you know is that you are here—through the clover, through the low-hanging branch, through the grapeshot.

All of it missed you.

Your saber is up, and there goes your head, Christian.

L I

I SEE no pressing reason to get out of bed. The lights are off and it is raining and the covers are the cave I dreamed of when I was a child. I am pretending to be sick—a faker like some of my patients. I dream of monsters that cannot get me. Ha ha. The covers touch me like mother hands. The memories of war talk in the house when I was growing up jabber around, and I close my eyes and bury my face in the pillow like little Ray of three. Bill and Elizabeth told me what an un-expected event I was, and that's how I feel to this day. Even I don't expect me. If I could happen, anything could.

Sister is knocking on the door, with a cry as dismal as when I first saw her in her funny gown on the railroad tracks.

Charlie DeSoto is knocking there too. He says he's got a new bow and arrow. My God, that in-terests me about as much as a traffic jam.

"You want to shoot some gar?" he says.

Westy was out of town. There was nothing else crazy to do. So we went. We went out High-way 82 to the swamps of the Sipsey River. And there the huge, rolling, scaly, comb-toothed, vi-cious-snouted gar were not waiting. We were over our shoes in mud, and it was drizzling dirty rain, getting chilly, and the water was as still as oil.

There was one woodpecker going-at it in the high branches of a dead tree. It was the only sign of life, and we'd been there two hours.

Charlie looked up at the woodpecker. Then he loaded the bow.

"Aw, Charlie," I said.

"If I don't kill something, I'm going to kill my wife," he said.

Says I, "Go ahead. You ain't going to hit it, anyway."

But he did. The arrow rose from the bow as dead-sure as a heat-seeker and skewered the lovely redheaded thing, went on up into the air with the bird still on it.

L I I

To live and delight in healing, flying, fucking. Here are the men and women.

L I I I

He waded, then swam. Then he came back the same way, sand and tears in his eyes. I say, "You must've been shooting that bow for a while."

"I been having hate in me since my wife turned lesbian or narcissistic or whatever," Charlie says. "But look, I've killed this beautiful bird. Ray, you've got to do something for me."

He looked like the creature of mud with a feather in his hand.

I have sympathy because a lot of the people I have loved and given to have never especially loved or given to me, and Westy is colding off like the planet, except I can't believe it in either case.

Nothing really to say except in some reaction like on the television.

Now I am looking at the bird with the arrow through it.

And all it does is make me very sleepy.

L I V

RAY meets Westy at the fancy yellow restaurant. She's looking pretty tired and old now. In the deep sparkling blue of her eyes I see a certain dangerous blank. Is Ray to blame? The rings and the other jewelry twinkle on her. I am looking at the other side of the hill now, at the sunken eyes, at the grim desperation of the earlobes. On her forehead Westy wears the wide frown of surrender.

"I am an old woman," says some voice.

"No no no no no no no," says mine.

"Ray, you care more about the sorriest scum than you do me."

"No, I don't," I say.

"Among your friends there is not one decent

straight solid person. They are entirely the mange, as far as I am concerned."

I say, "What about Charlie DeSoto? He wears a suit."

She just looked at me hopelessly.

"There is something about you, Ray, that wants to set yourself deliberately in peril and in trash. One of these days you won't come back alive. You are drinking again. You've had three vodka tonics."

I ordered a fourth. Some old hideous baby in me wanted to see Westy pissed.

"You lousy ignorant bitch," says Ray.

Westy got up and left, leaving me to bum a ride back to the office.

At the office there were a number of people in line. I went over to the back window and looked out over the creek, then down to it and the slick granite rocks through which it rushed. Who was it said we were invented by water as a means of its getting itself from one place to the other?

LV

I AM looking at the swelling hordes. I know too many goddamned people, too many wretched Americans at this point. Between the hours of healing, I dream of dropping the ace on much home real estate in hopes that many citizens will get trapped inside in the wide handshake of phosphorus.

Nothing wrong with me. For example, somebody's wife comes to see me. She says, Doctor, what's wrong? She says, I seem to have given all I can to make everybody comfortable, yet they despise me. All of my food and laundry elicits nothing but contempt in their eyes.

Back over in Mississippi my friend Wyatt Newman and I invented this girl that you took to the drive-in. She was rather large and leggy with huge breasts. During the movie she would start, after putting one hand to her brow, humping and moving her sex back and forth in motions of her inner time. She would sigh and pant. The fool who had dated her, skinny and never had any, would move over to touch her tits and give himself ease as well as affection to this large woman who was about to have to come over the whole idea of herself. But when he touches her, she knocks him away.

"Animal!" she screams.

Women are fucking awful. Sister was the one exception.

L V I

RAY is crawling this afternoon. Many things have broken down in our nice house. The only glory I see is the glory I saw as a jet fighter. I went

through the clouds and brought up the nose of the
Phantom, lifting at twenty-one hundred land miles
per hour. It was either them or me, by God. I
loved those clean choices. And I loved my jet. I
loved all those aerodynamics, the rising and diving.

Something's wrong.

Westy and I are not close in the old way. My
dreams are big discouraging monsters, hellish.
Had one that was a walking building, which was
my high school. It was my old high school chasing
me down the block.

I tell you, if not for his old records and his
Shakespeare, Ray would be a casualty of the
American confusion.

Like yesterday. Eileen, DeSoto's wife, wanted
to talk with me at the office. She was pale and she
had developed a dramatic deepness in her voice.
It was huskier, more Northern. I think she comes
from Selma, Alabama. I am not an expert on lesbianism, mind you.

"I want to describe what it is like, Ray," she
said.

I said, "First let me say that I am not an expert
on lesbianism."

"That's okay," she says, "I was shocked myself. I had fever and the shakes. It was like a big
dream where you can't help walking toward the
place although it's scary. There were a lot of
voices and mouths. Then I became one of the
mouths. I became one of the soft naked girls, and

an ecstasy ran through every part of my mind. And I was there at the place and it was familiar, like coming back to something you had as a child."

"Why'd you come see me?"

"Because you're a friend of Charlie's and he's very hurt. Besides, you are a doctor, aren't you?"

"Let me fuck you," I say. "It will be good for you. Doctor's orders," I say. "Come on," I say, "you crazy lesbian bitch—ohh, uhh, uhnn, touch it!"

L V I I

AND yet without a healthy sense of confusion, Ray might grow smug. It's true, isn't it? I might join the gruesome tribe of the smug. I think it's better with me all messed up.

I looked at the Nembutals this morning and thought for about three minutes about going over to the other side. Westy is snoring per usual. I love to hear her snore. I love to hear her come too. The whisper: "Aw, you made me come!" puts it out there like a pratfall, footing lost. If I could only get her to wear the high heels when she's nude, as in *Penthouse*. Going over to the other side, I'm not sure I could fuck, shoes or no. So I ditched the whole idea.

R A Y

Two thugs were looking for me when I got off work today.

Here's something.

"We got reason to believe you let our uncle die when he coulder been saved."

That old case several months ago. I was guilty.

"One of them nurses that was close to our family told us," said one guy.

"We going to make you a flat doctor," said the other one.

They were bikers and wore leather and studs and wrist guards. Two black-and-silver Harleys behind them. I felt very sleepy.

I said, "Yes. I let the old mean son of a bitch die." I was too tired to lie. I said, "Come on, boys. One of you will get hurt bad, but there are two of you." I was staring them down. They were huge, grimy creatures. The huger one was wearing a tattoo on his arm—skull and crossed swords.

Death is everywhere. Why do these killers on motorbikes think they have the corner on it?

"Come on," I said. "I'm full of death," I said. "Come and get it."

"Huh?" said the grimier thug. He was one of those hairy men who go out of their way to be ugly. His hair was to his shoulders and he had a bald spot on the top of his head.

"Yes!" I shrieked. "I come from the Navy and I know how to kill in a fight! One of you is going to get it. I don't right now have the energy but to kill one."

"Kill?"

"Come on!" I hollered. "Give it to me!" I took off my jacket.

They were not moving. Then they both moved fast and they slugged me around, mainly half-jabs to the belly. I never got a lick in and I fainted.

I guess this was justice in a way. I was sore when I came to, but to be truthful, I felt good. I was bleeding a little, but I felt fresh as sweet sixteen.

Such was my relationship with Westy at the time that she withdrew in disgust when I came home with the damage to my cheeks and forehead. There is a streak in some women that beats the shit out of a response to pain if the wounds are really sloppy. Even the old joys we knew could not abide against Westy's sense of the sanitary.

LIX

The thrill the suspense the spontaneity are
*   all hanging suspended by one ankle.*
There is one pompous tall bully I know.
Who shall be served.
He shall perish in the hot foam of his cruel
*   absurdity. He shall be boiled alive.*

RAY

His own power glide shall run him over.
His snide poems shall be twisted screw-wise up
* his organ's exit.*
Then we bring on the major stuff.
Rumors, backbiting, the hissing intimations.

That was a poem scratched out by yours truly when he had had a long season of no nooky. But now my loneliness is not preying on me as in the old days.

"What are you doing, Doctor?" says the new nurse.

"Writing a poem," says I. "Getting myself my own medicine."

"Oh," she says. "I always loved poetry absolutely to pieces!"

Here's some nooky, thinks I.

She was about twenty-three and the nurse's dress fit her okay. She was green-eyed, svelte, with ample bosom, etc. There wasn't the hard face of stupidity such as you see on most nurses. My eyes go to her feet and even there I see a bit of style. Some kind of trim-line whites showing a great deal of the fetching ankle and the blue veins Ray loves.

"I liked your lectures on nervous anxiety last year," says she.

I'm just grooving on those veins in her feet.

Says she, "Would you read me one of your poems? God, a doctor who writes poems."

"Let's fuck instead," says I. "What do we have?"

"Nothing. A couple of grown babies with runny noses. One of them's a woman who demands to see you personally."

"Who is it?"

"She's the suicidal Lebanese one that leases the Learjet through her law firm."

"Okay," I say, "we'll fuck tomorrow."

I pass by the mirror and see I'm still semihandsome. But you can never trust your own way of seeing.

L X

OVER Hanoi. Hendrix coming in clear. Coming down from high nowhere to blue somewhere to spy the water and the *Bonhomme Richard* in the luminous China Sea. There was a certain spirit that had the controls and guided me in to make the deck. It was the last of the last if you didn't. God bless America. At the last moment it is all spirit, because five things could go wrong before the hooks catch you and you are climbing out of the cockpit.

Oh, Captain, my Captain.

I saw the hospital in Hawaii. It turned my heart. I saw and heard them interviewing the wounded. The doctor goes in and asks a boy who's just lost a leg: "Do you feel different about life now?"

I need to hear Sister's voice.

Sister. Sister.

Ray is lucky. Ray can walk, think, and be a fool in his poems. I am lucky and I feel like fornication. Fellow doctor told me that there is some change and refreshment of hormones when you are with a lady overnight. Never knew that, but I will definitely study it for my long paper on the Nervous Anxiety of the Age.

Oh, God, my shirt isn't ironed! Etc.

Let us meet again, we with our gray and forward hats on a million horses. Pushing the attack toward Washington, D.C. Our loves have evaporated. We run counter to them. Looking at the vista, there are cavalrymen of every race and creed. There is the beauty of the horses, with a steam like cumulus rising from their nostrils. Are we in line?

"Raise sabers!" says the general.

Eventually every man's a sword. I'm riding down the lines and see Commander Gordon looking downcast. On myself I have the wool short jacket with every color of the rainbow on the breast.

"You haven't your saber, Commander. Raise it and you will see your men raise theirs."

"Sorry. I was thinking about my ex-wife. Brings

you down. I know I'm going to die and that brings me down."

"If you use the new pistol correctly, I don't think you'll die. We are about to launch the Air Force. Shoulders up, Commander! We've got every horse ready on its feet. We will race on water and then bring out the pistols. Every bullet is a heat-seeker. There's no use of my going through the book with you."

"Sabers up!" Commander Gordon says.

Behind him five thousand silver sabers rise.

"What do they have? What do their hired soldiers have?"

"We caught them short. All they have is the old lead. The machine guns. The air will bring down the potency of our jackets."

Christ, here we go. Not a chance, but what a territory to gain!

Their cannon just missed me as my horse started running on the water. We are high on our horses and laughing and I can hear the shrill Rebel yell behind me. They are throwing out phosphorus bombs, and I see some of the men go down. My men just laugh and the horses climb the banks. What an open field. We are laughing and screaming the yell.

It is an open field.

R A Y

IT was noon. I could not eat.

I went over to the Hooches because I knew the old man was off for a break from the tugboats.

Mr. Hooch was there and I caught him in the very act of writing. It was about Sister, his dead daughter and my dead lover.

In the ground my daughter is but should not be
My mind and face is coming strong toward
    victory
In the ground but better her singing for the
    worms
Than the town and all of its terms
Below what happened, she lies, in no disguise
My daughter always loved the earth anyway
And when I put my ear to live grass I can hear
    her
I can hear her, I can hear her, I can hear her.
And when I stand up I am dirty in my veins
I am soiled throughout. That's Sister
Mister.

He took a Kool off me. I was humiliated by his poetry and I had to go to the bathroom to cry loud. It was a storm of tears.

Sister was with me. "Keep on, Doctor," she said.

His wife came out and gave me a nod.

When I think I'm doing good, I have to come over and see that I'm not even in the contest. In fact I have put the old fart in contact with an English prof at the school, who's also a poet. It seems that the *Collected Poems* of J. Hooch are going to be a published fucking reality.

I was laboring on another one when that new nurse came in again. She was quite a choice and I was out of nooky going on four months. For some weird reason I began lying to her lavishly. They were not harmful lies. I invented a whole new biography and person. I get tired of being him, Ray, all the time.

"And so when I jumped out of the U-2 and saw all the Chinese around me, I knew there had been a misreckoning on someone's part. Instead of killing me, however, they were friendly, knew that I was a doctor in training, and introduced me to all the ins and outs of acupuncture. I guess I began to write poems about then."

"Wow. Do you ever write about sex?"

"Often," I replied.

"Does anyone ever get enough sex?" she asked.

"The spring in me is very tight. Nothing else will do except gigantic fucking and sucking. ing."

"Are you speaking poetry to me now?"

SOUNDED like something. It was in cold weather. From my heart I follow the ghost voice. It is leading me and leading me and leading me.

Oh, my! Oh fortunate fool! It is the voice of Westy and she wants to screw. I adore a woman who shouts for screwing. I adore! What with her legs in the air! What with her coming! What with her cheer and despair together!

Close your eyes, darling, and have the old original pleasure! Tongue in, tongue out. Big hard sexuals.

Ah, my God, you've made me come!

Everyone thinks it's a crisis at sunrise, but I do not. I think of rising in the Phantom at dawn and the dawn intense—orange, yellow, violet, blueblack—the day very present because it could be the day of your death.

Westy lifted her legs around me. She wanted to see the old miracle of my big thing going in.

What a paradise of delight marriage can be.

Nothing comes close to Westy in the pussy department.

And you can see how my poetry is improving.

I'm climbing the high oak of learning.
I'm feeling the old force of yearning.

Hoo! Ray! Fucking Ray! Ray in the fourth decade!

Ray, yes, Ray! Doctor Ray is okay!

Charlie DeSoto and Eileen are together again. The nurses are getting married. Westy is coming with the hot oils and the balm. The Alabama team is still whipping everybody in sight. My patients are calling. Bill is getting ready to fish. Elizabeth is looking in the Holy Bible. Mr. Hooch has his hands on a pencil.

Sister!

Christians!

Sabers, gentlemen, sabers!

Barry Hannah was born in Clinton, Mississippi, thirty-eight years ago. He was awarded the William Faulkner Prize for his first novel, *Geronimo Rex.* A second novel, *Nightwatchmen,* was followed by *Airships,* a collection of stories brought out by Knopf as an Arnold Gingrich Short Fiction Award. His achievement in fiction was recently honored by the American Academy of Arts and Letters.

A NOTE ON THE TYPE

This book was set in a modern adaptation of a type designed by the first William Caslon (1692–1766), greatest of English letter founders. The Caslon face, an artistic, easily read type, has had two centuries of ever-increasing popularity in our own country—it is of interest to note that the first copies of the Declaration of Independence and the first paper currency distributed to the citizens of the newborn nation were printed in this type face.

The book was composed by American–Stratford Graphic Services, Inc., Brattleboro, Vermont, and printed and bound by The Haddon Craftsmen, Inc., Scranton, Pennsylvania

Designed by Dorothy Schmiderer